Kandy 2

RISE OF JAH'MES EMPIRE

JEREMY JAE-JAE DAVIS

Jeremy Jae Jae Davis

ISBN: 9798814493613

Printed in the United States of America

Copyright © 2022 by Jeremy "Jae-Jae" Davis

Library of Congress control number 2022905504

Uptownclassic757@gmail.com

The projects were rolling and money was coming in by the bundles. Jah'me and his street team of hustlers, had the streets of Norfolk and certain sections of the Beach on lock for the past year, their new connects supply was so potent they could easily put a four on it! And numbers never lie because Jah'me and his crew brought in almost a "Hundred Grand" this week.

The crew would always meet up at Jah'mes luxury condo to discuss their weekly income. It didn't matter if they took a loss or gained a profit, "money was always the topic. Suddenly the smell of Versace Blue Jeans cologne overwhelmed room. He sported a gold "Richard Mille fly back wrist watch, an all white casual polo shirt, bucket hat and a pair of all white ones. "He addressed his crew. what's "good "my People? " Whats up? They all replied back!

The last time I checked we, "been getting money! our rents are paid and our families straight. "Facts! Cuzzo added back. Cuzzo was the baby boy of the crew, he and Wing were both, Jah'mes cousins they all grew up together uptown. Wing was their "Enforcer" He kept everything balanced," you need a nigga like him In your crew, "he had no problem putting you" in your place or in the trunk.

Rob was Jah'mes best friend, you could never catch him out without his ace and vise versa.

Their Hussle started back in the early ninety's where they attended "Ruffner a popular middle school in Norfolk, VA. "Every morning they would stop pass the local Shop-N-Go to steal gum, sunflower seeds, soda's and candy.

"They would then go to the designated spot to count the inventory, price each item, add it all up, make the sales to the "kids in class, and meet back up, As soon as the bell rings and split the "profit.

"They soon progressed to selling weed, which didn't last long due to their shopping and smoking habits. They needed something different. They all agreed to sell heroin and "crack something they promised to one another, to never indulge in. "Their journey trust and loyalty goes way" back to the sandbox ! And continue throughout the following years,,,,,,

 PJ was the popular one of the crew, "he was a prominent rising basketball star, with the likes of Duke, NC, and Michigan kicking down his door!

One night his girlfriends baby father came over all high on Percocet and drunk on some other shit"! a scuffle broke out between the two of them, and

PJ was charged with malicious "wounding, He did three-years and was released on Christmas Eve. Happy to be home, but bittersweet. A thirty second decision had just changed the course of his entire life...

" I got tickets to the Buju Bonton concert at the Nova tonight" Jah'me said. Count me in "phew" Cuzzo replied. " I have to make a couple of runs, but I will let you know something! PJ seconded.

They all got up, ready to leave for the mall. And since we had a "hellava" week everything's on me, Jah'me said. In that case count me in PJ excitedly chanted". No! nigga you dead, Like you said you got shit to do "phew" Jah'me taunted.

After leaving Macarthur Mall Cuzzo asked, Jah'me if he could make a stop to "McDonald's? why you didn't eat out of the food court fam? "He asked. Last time I checked my "bitch was back at the crib! Cuzzo replied with a slick tone.

OH yeah! and if I'm not mistaken your car is back at the crib too, along with your "poe ass "bitch! we ain't stopping no where "dick head! Jah'me yelled over the music blasting through the speakers in his luxury ride.

Well at least stop at the store, I got all this gas and no fucking "blunts, he said inhaling the blueberry aroma of the Kush.

I'll stop at Shop-N-Go once we get Up-Town and you can order you some of that nasty ass pizza. You crazy! Cuzzo replied "back I eat it everyday, that shit a missile "phew."

Let me asked you something" Have you ever seen them "Arabs wash they hands or even use sanitizer? "hell no! explained Jah'me. And to make matters even worse" they handle the money too! Look at your face now! Yo "uck" mouth pizza eating azz!

They all burst out laughing. This was always their vibe. To any outsider, those were fighting words, But to them. They were just shooting the breeze, cruising through the town. And getting a little money of course……

THE Shop-N-Go up-town was always packed you were liable to see anybody and everybody either coming or going. It was the same store the rap duo, The Clipse" shot their music video "Grinding! And a host of uptown legends could be seen posted up at times.

Cuzzo returned back to the car super excited. "Yo, it's a "chic so fine and thick in that damn line ace! How thick? Jah'me asked. Because their definition of thick was definitely different. He would always have Cuzzo compare his women celebrity's. Ok she got a face like "H.E.R and a azz like "Megan the stallion! Cuzzo described.

"Say word Rob replied, we have to see Her, minutes later a female who fit that description emerged from the store. "Their she go! Said cuzzo. "Damn!!! They yelled in union. Go get her! Jah'me instructed. Rob exited the car and approached the sexy female, For a second she looked interested, then she shook her head no, and began to slowly back away.

Jah'me could easily read her body language, so he rolled down the tinted window of his Mercedes Benz and said, "excuse me. I see you have a box of blunts in your hand, you trying to match "one, two, or "three? He said with a gentle smile.

I have to find some "weed first. She replied back. We got all the weed you can smoke baby, Cuzzo yelled from the back seat holding up an ounce, come get in.

Only if I can take a picture of y'all license plate. "Fuck no! Jah'me said, you a fly chic" but we ain't on it like that! He "boldly stated. It's just for my safety, I'm not on it like that neither, but I am a female and y'all are three "deep she calmly stated.

Well since you put it like that, I understand. After

snapping the picture, She entered the car and sat directly behind Jah'me, he quickly adjusted his rear view to get a better look, Liking what he observed, he asked what's your name beautiful and where are you from? I'm "Kandy from North Carolina, I'm just here for the summer. So who are you some kin too around here? Rob asked.

"Nobody you would know, my auntie is older and she been sick for awhile, so I'm kind of helping her out until she gets better.

That's what's up Jah'me replied. So you trying to ride and smoke? It's whatever but who's car is this? Why? Rob asked. Just asking it's nice. Thank you! Jah'me replied. I guess you know who car it is now Cuzzo said rolling his back wood.

How old are you Kandy? I'm "twenty-two. Gat Damn" you "phat as hell" to be in your early twenties! Cuzzo said looking serious. Kandy had never laughed so hard in her life! she found him to be quite amusing. That's just country eating baby, she replied back.

For now on, my bitch eating turkey necks, collar greens and potatoes everyday! He ranted on.

We have to find a duck off spot to blow at! "Up-Town is on fire right now! The DT's and narc's been lurking every day since that "missile dope hit the streets Jah'me added. I have a room at the Economy Lodge we can go their, if y'all down. We definitely down with that Rob agreed, at that very moment they gave each other the look" the "we fucking look."

 Michelle was an uptown girl who had been dealing with Jah'me for years on and off, their relationship was purely sexual. She was leaving the beauty supply store, when she spotted his Benz parked, at the motel. She proceeded to park next to it and called his phone.

"Yo he answered? "Boy who you got up in that room with you? that's about to get her azz" dragged!! He peeped out the window and existed room.

Michelle stood standing beside his car with her lip poked out and arms folded as he approached. Look Michelle don't be coming up here tripping like you my woman or something. I'm trying to take care of some business. So miss me wit all this! where the hell you coming from anyways? he asked.

 The beauty supply store. okay bout to get that knotty head done up he said jokingly. I wanted the Africans to do it but they charge an arm and a leg. But they do a good job Jah'me said passing her three hundred dollars, and don't get them braided down to your "ankles I hate that shit. I won't baby just to the middle of my "back, ok sounds good to me. thanks boo! Your welcome now Let me handle this and I'll call you when I'm done. Make sure you do that, she replied back getting in her Acura and driving away.

Jah'me walked back into the room and too his surprise "Kandy and "Cuzzo was in the bathroom fucking! Damn what I miss that quick? he asked Rob. I have a clue it happened so fast bro, he said back!

What the hell you was doing that you missed that play? Jah'me asked laughing. I was smoking and checking my stocks from yesterday. Man stock that nigga out that "bathroom ace. You already know lil cuzz fuck like rabbit bro, he should be done in a couple minutes! Rob said laughing, while throwing back two double shots of Hennessy.

"Cuzzo exited the bathroom ten minutes later, sweating bullet's! Rob entered with a box of Magnums in his hands, along with Jah'me, it wasn't the first time they had ran a train on a female, that was just something they did.

At certain times Kandy seemed more comfortable than they were, they couldn't believe how someone could have let this pretty yet "freaky "azz girl get away!

What the crew didn't know was that Kandy had just recently been released from doing a five year stretch at Fulton F.C.C. federal prison for women. Her well proportioned "voluptuous body and younger looks! defined that.

Kandy was actually from the Up-Town section of the city, But it had been awhile since she had been their, everyone she knew or remembered were either in jail, dead, or had relocated.

"She knew she looked totally different and nobody would recognize her. "Her only mission was to find a young "Hustler she could manipulate and set-up to get her boyfriend out of prison. The Fed's called it a "Downward Departure, and if she did it right" He could walk out of prison a free man.

Trey was a Portsmouth Hustler who had a pass to Hussle Up-Town. That's when the Town Point Motel was like the "Carter and money was plentiful a solid thirty day run and you were Rich."

He kept good fish scale and a "missile dope that could stand a three. The hustlers and dope "fiends all loved him. He got crossed up Fucking with Killer, and Dez, hot asses and was given a life sentence......

Jah'me sat up and rolled up another blunt, he couldn't believe how beautiful she was. Kandy walked out of the shower with just a towel wrapped around her wet body, Come over here Kandy! Jah'me said tapping the bed.

What's good? She asked. "You he confidently responded, you trying to get down with my team? This was the opportunity she had been waiting for, of course was her instant reply.

We're young but we focused! You already know, we getting to the bag! But most of all we're "loyal to one other! "Not the streets. We operate in a tight circle, no square's allowed. We're the N.F.L team! What does that mean she asked? drying her naked body as if they were the only two in the room. "It means we niggas for life! Cuzzo overheard the conversation and added in,

We tackle the block and fumble through ho's and touch down money like the mutherfucker pro's!! He yelled out staggering to the bathroom. "Facts all facts that boy a fool, Jah'me said laughing.

Do you have your driver's license? Of course that's mandatory, as much as I hate walking, she responded. You can be my driver is that cool? I'm cool with whatever you need me to do Jah'me!

"Well shit In the meantime climb your lil-thick azz

in this bed and suck on this dick again, wit your cute azz! Licking her lips she replied back, I was hoping you would say that!

A loud "knock on the room door woke the three of them What the "fuck? Cuzzo shouted! reaching for Rob's gun, room service! Fresh towels and sheets, sir!" we good! Cuzzo yelled. check out is in a hour the maid informed.

Jah'me rolled over from his deep sleep, he was drained from sexing Kandy all night.

A where did she go "nephew? Rob shouted! Jah'me immediately jumped up and started checking his pockets. The rest of the crew followed suit. They all had their jewelry cash and drugs. Cuzzo looked out of the window and noticed the Benz was missing. Oh "shit Bro! she stole the whip! Jah'me ran to the window.

"Damn we knew better staying the night, we got caught slipping ace! But why she didn't take all of our shit? I don't understand Rob said shaking his head, it's well over a "hundred-grand worth of jewelry and money on the table.

Just when they thought she was gone in the wind, they heard Jah'mes Bose sound system pulling into the hotel parking lot. Their she go, bro! "Cuzzo yelled. Man Im going to mush the hell out of her ass, Jah'me said storming out the room.

"Kandy had changed into a sexy short Jean skirt, a wife beater, two gold chains, gold hoop earrings, and wheat timberlands. What's your problem taking my shit? Jah'me asked. Kandy continued to dance seductively to the lady saw sycamore tree song, as if he wasn't say anything worth hearing.

 She reached into the car and pulled out a several bags of food from Shoney's. I left the note on top of the TV Daddy! She looked up and seen Rob and Cuzzo peeping out the door. Can you come and help me with this breakfast, I stopped at Walmart too and brought you all some fresh boxers and tee shirts.

Thank you, but that note better be on that TV Jah'me said in a serious tone. As soon as he stepped back into the room, he noticed a piece of paper on top of the television,

It read,, Daddy since I'm officially on the team, I'm going to play my position and make sure the crew straight. I'm going to freshen up then get breakfast for us all. The time now is nine o' clock, I won't be gone long, I'll be back before eleven o' clock check -out. Jah'me looked down at his Rolex and it read ten fifteen. Kandy had just solidified her place with his crew.

Kandy had learned from Kesha back in the days that anytime she stayed at a motel she always had two rooms. *You just never know who or what could possibly return to hurt or Robb you Kandy nighazs is* crazy. Those were the words Kesha said that forever stuck with her. She actually just drove his car on the other side of the motel where she had another room with all of her belongings.

Kandy was well seasoned she had been around "Hustlers her entire life, she already knew the Hussle game and what Jah'me expected out of her, and she planned on doing just that. So far so good, she said to herself, plotting and scheming..

Jah'me had two spot's doing numbers. On this particular Sunday evening he Kandy and Cuzzo sat at Feather n Fin eating chicken sandwiches, while waiting on the call to pick up the profits, his trap house had brought in for the week. Something just don't feel right, Jah'me said looking around, it's too quiet out today. pull around to Manson Street Kandy.

It's super "dead out this Bitch! "Cuzzo added looking around. Kandy continued driving they all noticed the "narc's parked on the corner, and right beside a stop sign at that! She had no other choice but to stop, giving them a full access look into the vehicle.

"shit y'all fall back and spray the blunt out! Kandy instructed. Jah'me and Cuzzo buckled their seat belts and slouched into their seats. "Kandy watched her rearview, as the "narc's pulled out behind her. She kept her composure as she drove into the nice neighborhood, noticing that she was being tailed, she quickly pulled into a drive way and exited the car.

"Hello officers she greets! as they slowly drove by. she walked up to the strange house and ringed the door bell, A female answered the door. May I help you? Yes, does "Antwan live here? No I'm sorry he don't, the older woman replied. Kandy gave her a confused look but thanked the lady before heading back to the car.

Once back in the car Kandy buckled her seat belt y'all good?" For show! Cuzzo added. So Daddy where too? She asked. Back "uptown he replied, this shit hot as fish "grease. At that moment he said to himself I'm really starting to feel this "chic.

Back at the hotel, Kandy received a collect call. "Heey "Baebeee! She bellowed. What's "happening" he replied. You putting that work in for your man or what?" I'm doing what I can I've only been home three week's, you got to give me some time "bae!

I then gave these crackers five years and your

stupid ass talking about more time. "Nigga watch your mouth I'm not that little girl you Can manipulate anymore. I'm going to help you because I love you, but you have to be patient!

My "agent said he just need something concrete, so make sure they are caught "dirty with "guns, "heroin or "crack, bae! Trey informed her. Can you please stop talking like that over the phone, she cautioned him. My bad, but I need you to handle that for me "ASAP! I love you were his last words before the phone hung up.

I bet you do Kandy said to herself, she realized that his only mission was to get out and do him again, he didn't love her, he just wanted to use her to get his ass free. In some ways she felt obligated to help him, because he took good care of her outside of jail, but at the end of the day, when she was in jail he left her for "dead, no "lawyer, no money, no "commissary, and not once in their conversation had he asked, how she was doing?

"Jah'me was different, He brought her nice things and took her places without cursing her out and beating on her every other day. She knew in her heart that Jah'me was a "good man, she couldn't do him dirty like that! she could easily see herself being his better half, after careful "contemplation she said "fuck Trey! let his "grimy ass rot in jail where he belongs, She was finally over him.

"Michelle called Jah'mes phone, he answered on the second ring. What's good? You! she replied back walking back and forth in her bra and boy shorts, smoking a blunt." What happened to you Sunday night? I looked all over for your ass!

You didn't look hard enough because I was backstage! He replied back. That's fucked up Jah'! You know I'm crazy about "Buju Banton! I know! that's why I got you an autograph. I don't believe you liar! She said laughing, I know you and you have never been a groupie! Well I was for you last night he replied.

So what you doing now? She asked. "shit chilling why? Because I'm high and Horney you know what that means. She taunted. No I don't! He replied back. I wanna "fuck "nigga! Bad timing he replied back" Come on Jah' I know you have shit to do. I'm not going to hand cuff you. I just want some dick and you can leave. you always say that "shit Michelle and when I get their you get the tripping and never let me leave.

Im going to let you leave Jah' I promise, I started my night shift tonight anyways at One Stop! Which one he asked? Princess Ann Cross from "Park Terrance". Don't be lying Michelle. I swear

Jah' I have to be to work by ten o clock. Jah'me couldn't resist Her "missile head! just give me a hour I'll be through. Okay I'll see you then she replied.

Two hour's later Jah'me pulled up at Michelle's apartment along with Kandy driving. I'm only going to be an hour so don't go far. He looked at his watch and added, call my phone at seven-thirty sharp.

Yes daddy she replied back looking mean and sexy at the same time. Jah'me really liked Kandy but after she let his crew run a train on her, he couldn't even look at her passionately. To him she was just his "driver Why you so quiet?" he asked. You haven't talked the entire ride over, you need to tell me something? No everything is "okay daddy, she replied back with a awkward smile.

Jah'me was a born energy reader and could tell something wasn't right, he figured she was just jealous, knowing he was about to "fuck another woman, Kandy watched as Jah'me knock on the door only to be welcomed in by a short, "fimilure looking light skinned woman. As soon as he walked inside, she pulled off. Jah'me liked the fact that she waited, he reminded himself to take a note of that! "Cuzzo, Rob, and everyone he could think of always pulled off before he entered. He

19

was starting to see that "Kandy was just a different breed.

"Kandy wanted to tell Jah'me that she had just come home from doing a "bid, and that she was originally from "Up-Town, and how she got caught up in that "Trey mess thinking she was being loyal and Riding for her man.

she wanted to express how bad she wanted to start over and to be his "Ryder. but she knew from being in prison that a lot dirt had been thrown on her name involving "Trey, Daz, and "killer being incarcerated.

She hated the fact that he was fucking other bitches in front of her, when she knew she was the total package. she was determined to win him over, some way, some how, but she knew she had to come clean.

Wing received a call that Their new York connect had gotten tore off on the New Jersey Turnpike and wouldn't be able ship the crew their monthly supply any longer.

Just when Jah'me was about to get some head, his phone rings He noticed it was his cousin Wing, I have to answer this! Michelle rolled her eyes and sucked her teeth while getting up to get her a shot of "tequila, she preferred to be drunk anyways it gave her an excuse to be extra "Freaky blaming it all on the alcohol.

"So you telling me the connect dead and stinking "nephew? Jah'me asked Wing. Like Elmo Jenkins he rhythmically responded.

Damn just when shit was getting good, Jah'me vented. So all we have left is the income coming in from "dirty Felicia spot, the two "barber shops and the "penitentiary's ? Yep I'm on my way to pay the C/O's now for the next run, bet hit me back and let me know how that go cuzzo!

Jah'me laid his phone down on the "couch as Michelle unzipped his pants, and began to deep throat him with her long wet tongue.

Jah'me laid back closes his eyes and enjoyed the feeling. And that's when she made her move, "Michelle reached over and turned his phone off, she only had an hour and was determined to get every last minute. But to her surprise! at Seven-thirty-five their was a loud "knock at the front door!!!

Who the hell knocking on my door like the "fucking police? Michelle yelled!! She opened the door and "Kandy was standing their in her tight jeans, her hair in a ponytail with her Jordans sneakers on, holding her purse. "Is Jah'me here? she asked.

Why? Was Michelle's immediate response. Because I'm here to "pick him up! She "agressively retorted.

Jah'me overheard their conversation and quickly interrupted it. Michelle this is my driver Kandy" Your driver? Kandy sarcastically repeated back. "Yeah! my driver like I said. Why didn't you call my phone like I told you? I did, but it just kept going to your voice voicemail. So I came over and I didn't come alone.

He looked of the window thinking she had brought his crew along. She smirked and pulled out a baby 380. "Girl put that shit away before you hurt yourself " you changed clothes and everything, coming over here ready to rumble, you terrible Kandy he said laughing.

He looked at his phone. Michelle turned my phone off again! thanks for your concern though, I fucks with you the long way for that! "Anytime Daddy!" and why the "fuck she calling you daddy? Michelle jealously asked. Because I'm her "daddy. That's why! He told her walking out. "Call me! She managed to say before he got into his Benz. Jah'me shook his head and asked Kandy to take him Up-Town.

Michelle wasn't a spring chicken at all, she was

well seasoned and five years older than Jah'me. She had made a name for herself from "boosting. She kept all of the latest fashion's from clothes, shoes, jackets, and expensive cologne's. And if she didn't have it, she could get it in a matter of minutes.

Jah'me met her on a cold rainy week day, He was going into "Dillard's to grab a few things and waste some time. After several minutes of shopping he was approached by "Michelle, shaking her head like he had done something wrong.

You bout to buy all of that? she said pointing at the pile of clothes on his shoulders. "Yeah why? He asked. You work here or something? She added it all up in her head and said that's about a good six hundred you about to spend. IT probably is he replied back "sumthin light! He said in a cocky tone. I can give you all of that for three fifty right now! and I will throw in your favorite cologne, just tell me your size and take my number, I'll call and meet you anywhere but here she said.

Bet Jah'me said excited giving her his math, and I like Nautica, polo, curve, preferably "Versace Blue Jeans. I got you she replied back! And every since that day, Michelle was his go to when it came to getting fresh gear. she never got him what everyone else was rocking at that time, he was different and she recognized that!!

 She also recognized that woman that popped up knocking on her door, she remembered she used to boost for "Trey out in Portsmouth, and she look exactly like his "girlfriend Racheal who told on him and took down his boy's killer, and Jack..

Back at the spot Jah'me called a meeting and had everyone show. Just so y'all know, we don't have Fat Tony to supply us anymore. I was told Wing, that he got busted by the Fed's on the turnpike I be telling y'all all the time, that turnpike dangerous as hell especially when you're shaking and moving.

So with that being said, we have to find another way to bringing in some change, until we can find another route or another connect that's fair niggas Killing the game with these numbers at thirty-eighth

Kandy had developed a love like no other for Jah'me, she loved his leadership, his loyalty, and most of all his ambition. she decided she would try and put him on with her uncle "Donte, she had just recently connected back with him and he told her whatever she needed he would supply, she had that spot reserved for Trey but now she wanted nothing more than for Jah'me to have it. "Daddy, may I speak with you in private?" she asked. "Yeah Y'all hold up! he said.

What's up with that "daddy shit? He ain't no damn "pimp!" Cuzzo added. Rob began to laugh, "don't aske me "nigga!

Back in the kitchen Kandy revealed that she had a uncle in Washington DC who played in the NFL, and he had a huge portion of the drug market on the east coast smash. And she could give him a call, She knew whatever his prices were she could get em for the low. Damn that's wassup Kandy I need a blessing like that right about now he said excited.

"Kandy entered the living room minutes later revealing, that her uncle said he would do it, they just had to take a road trip. Jah'me decided he would take a "Quater Mill in cash, first impressions is a mutherfucker! He said unloading his safe.......

The road trip was three hours. "man that weather man lied! "Cuzzo said looking at out of the window. Jah'me was high eating chips, locked" in on a old Floyd Mayweather fight he had missed. can you even see Kandy? Yeah a little bit! "She replied. "This shit is getting worse though, We might need to pull over or find the closest motel.

The sign read gas, food, and lodging next five miles. Jah'me decided to find a room for the night the weather was terrible and he wasn't planning on being stuck on nobody's side of the road with a quarter mill in the trunk.

The Day's Inn was newly built and the rooms were definitely up to par, Jah'me requested a "presidential suite for the night being the Boss he was, the suite had a full living room kitchen, three bedrooms, and a seventy-five inch flat screen television, they all gathered down stairs where they continued to watch the fight.

Cuzzo saw that Kandy was all up under Jah'me most of the night so he decided to leave. Soon after Kandy confessed to Jah'me that she was falling in love with him, hearing this revelation he couldn't help but to laugh. But Daddy I'm serious! But how? he asked. I don't know I just am!" she explained in her baby voice. "Make love to me, she added kissing on his neck. "make love to me" she repeated. She stripped azz naked, making it damn near impossible for him to resist.

The beautiful neighborhood was lined with nothing but Luxury estates, "Damn now this is the life, my nigga! Cuzzo said, admiring the beautiful estates they passed by, once at the end of the street they embarked upon a big steel gate, you couldn't see beyond the gate or the tall brick walls, but you knew that something behind it was extremely nice.

Hello how can I help you the voice on the intercom interjected. I'm Kandy, Donte's niece! Hello Kandy he is expecting your arrival! The gate open and their eyes bugged in amazement, this nigga "Donte was loaded, his drive way alone was crazily lined with Bentley's, Phantoms, Benzes, he even had four wheelers just sitting on his lawn fitted with twenty-six inch rims, and The estate itself resemble a "shopping mall.

Good evening how was the ride up? The butler asked. It's was ok Kandy replied. He took their jackets , You are expected in the west wing go down the hall and take the first right. Good looking Jeffery! Cuzzo said before he tipped the butler five dollars.

Now remember Jah' we've been together for five years. I told my uncle that you been the only one who has been taking care of me, and that you dropped your connect because of his high numbers, She reminded him. Sounds good to me! he replied. Who is your uncle anyways? he asked walking around admiring the house. "Donte Nixon! Word from the Town played for Booker T ? Yep that's him.

Kandy!! "Donte said walking in. It's so good to see

you, uncle "Dee! She screamed, Kandy had turned back into a little girl as she hugged her uncle.

Wow! It's been so long! He said. And you look just like china too, all beautiful and stuff. Is this the lucky man? He motioned at Jah'me.

"Yes it is. This is my man Jah'me, it's a pleasure to meet you "king! I'm her uncle, she has always been my favorite niece, he said hugging Kandy. Can u excuse us for a minute Kandy? Ok unk! I'm going to show Cuzzo the car collection.

Jah'me would you like a drink? Donte offered. Yeah! why not? Brown or white? Brown Jah'me added. Good choice, you can always tell the character of a man by what he drinks.

Oh yeah" I never knew that Jah'me replied, I just so happen to like "Hennessy. Donte started laughing. So what brings you, my way Jah'me? "Donte asked. Im here to get some quality work for a fair price. How long you been with my niece? About a couple of Days, we just met, but she thorough and I fucks with her the long way! I like you Jah'me, Kandy told me you all been together for five years, but I know she just like to put her dope boys friends on, she loves to be pampered. Thank you for keeping it solid, you're a man of good "character, That's something you don't see much of now a days!

No amout of money or drugs could ever change me! That's all I know how to be ace! Not trying to throw her under the bus or nothing, but in this game "loyalty and "trust is all we have. Jah'me said. "Absolutely "Donte replied. I have people's lives I'm managing, can't risk my name and integrity for nothing.

  Can you tell me a little bit about yourself? Of course I'm twenty got a couple legit businesses, I just opened my third "barber shop in "Norfolk, and I'm looking forward to opening up a few car lots out the way with my man PJ. I'm definitely not trying to be in these streets my whole life, I just want to be able to make enough paper to build my brand and to take care of my team properly, so that one day we all can be in a situation similar to yours. Well the "Harvest is definitely "plentiful", Donte said opening his million dollar drapes, revealing his "fleet of luxury cars and manicured lawn.

You speak highly of your team. you know it's always a weak link in every crew! "Donte said. That's what they say. Replied Jah'me. I'm more into hustling with family and friends that I've knowned from the sandbox, it's different when your moving that way...

"Donte walked back towards the window and saw Cuzzo, admiring his wraith, he been looking at my car for a minute, he definitely going to get him one. Hell yeah Jah'me said laughing, he love riding luxury with little Charlie Faulk money! they both burst out laughing. But all jokes aside that's my baby cousin, and I'm going to make it much easier for him to get it whenever the opportunity presents itself.

Well that just may be sooner than you think, because I have a shipment coming in today and it's well over a "hundred kilos, I can give them to you for "twenty a brick!! That sounds like music to my ears "Donte!!

I brought a " quarter million with me, Jah'me opened the three duffle bags revealing the stacked bundles of hundreds. You can keep that, this first shipment I'm fronting you on consignment you're a "rare breed. This shipment should makes you an instant millionaire if done right, I see the greatness in you and it's a pleasure to be doing business with you, enjoy that money and make sure you buy my niece something nice her birthday coming up. No doubt I got you and I "appreciate everything too "Donte.

You might have to hang around for the next couple hours, I will call your phone when the shipment arrives, you just have to show up at the location on time! Kandy should know her way around pretty well. But this will be our first and final time meeting. I'm a pro football player and I try my best to keep my dirt on the low.

This is "Dave the man you will be networking through, I will make sure I go over everything with him. But until you hear from me! everything is always going be, what it is, You family now Jah'me, but remember it's always a weak link in every chain, every crew, mobb or "organization but live niggas stay on point "Factz Jah'me added. they both shook hands and "Donte exited , along with his two butlers and one maid.

Jah'me was going to go shopping in DC until the shipment arrived. Y'all ready we about to go spend some money! Damn right Cuzzo replied.

Jah'me decided to called PJ and Wing back at the home front. What's good Jah'? You already know my Gee. I scored a "hunndid of them"janks! The "fuck outta here wing shouted! All facts, Jah'me replied back just as excited. Look I'ma need you to get all the spots up and running make sure you pay "dirty Falichia rent, were definitely going to need her spot to cut and cook this work. PJ you hit everybody in the prison's and let them know the work and Jack's are on the way! I got it Jah'me you just drive home safe my Gee, I'll see your "rich ass, as soon as you get here, our rich asses Jah'me corrected him asap, we a team ace! Yeah you know I know the count Wing said.

Cuzzo was the most excited he couldn't wait to cop a rental and dog it out on the interstate. he wasn't trying to be around Kandy and Jah'me boo loving all fucking day! Alright Cuzzo don't go far. You definitely don't know your way around here. Jah' I got this bro, I saw a luxury car lot, on Bell View parkway on the way here, I just want to check out some" fly whips.

Cool me and Kandy are going to go and cop some jewelry I'll catch up with you later.

Kandy and Jah'me had time to talk, I just wanted to thank you for putting me on with the connect, "Donte good people's.

Yeah Kandy replied I can tell he likes you too! How Jah'me asked? Because he never talks that much I was out their talking to Cuzzo crazy ass for over an hour.

He values his time, did everything go well? Yes it did He said to give him a couple of hours, so we not going to listen to the radio or watch TV until I get that call, cool with me Kandy said looking out of the window.

Kandy was just about to tell him the truth about her past until PJ called all excited!

At the jewelry store Jah'me brought Kandy a pink ten carat cuban link diamond necklace. A pink ten carat bracelet. And a pink ten carat princess cut diamond earring set. It's set him back thirty five thousand, he never once showed it to Kandy" because her birthday was coming soon, he advised the jeweler to keep it on the low.

He then saw a diamond pinky ring that took his breath away! Can I get a discount for the ring? Of course the jeweler added, ten grand. Bet! Jah'me excitedly accepted. The price tag said twenty-two, he also purchased "Richard Millie's for his whole crew, by the time he left, he had spent well over a "hundred and "fifty thousand easy! Cuzzo called and asked him to drive up to the lot to check out the cars with him.

As soon as they pulled up they noticed Cuzzo sitting in a all black Bentley Gt Coupe sitting on black twenty-two inch wheels. You like he asked? Yeah that shit crazy "Cuzzo Jah'me replied. He only want "eighty-grand I got to have this in my life Jah'me. But Cuzzo you be driving on suspended license regularly, and it's no way you going to drive that "Up-Town and not get pulled ace!

Ok I hear you! I'm going to get my license straight but I need you to bless me with this car Cuzz!

 I've always bless you, I gave you the Acura Legend, the MPV, the 300z, two Q45s how much you want to be blessed with my nigga! A Bentley bitch! cuzzo yelled back laughing. That's when when we were poe, I want a rich nigga car now ya digg? Boy if you wasn't my cousin Jah'me retorted. you gotta find somewhere to park it, like a house my nigga!, Or the condo I'm moving in next month, cuzzo replied back.

Just then a younger looking man in a suit walked up, how can I help you guys? "How much u want for this "Bentley? Jah'me asked. I'll take "eighty-grand! He replied. How many miles she got? One hundred and ten. And how many owners. One the dealer replied. But these type of vehicles are made for the road and mileage. "Is that right? Do you have "phantoms or "wraiths? Of course." the dealer replied. I'm sorry I didn't get your name. Jah'me asked. I'm Luke he replied back shaking his hand, pleases to meet you Luke.

 Luke had a new respect for Jah'me. He knew he wasn't just a tire kicker, from looking at   This young man he knew Jah'me was strictly about his business.

They all walked around to the back garage where Luke revealed two beautiful Phantoms parked beside one another, one white and the other was red.

"Damn this shit nasty! Jah'me said. " it's going for two "hundred thousand Luke stated. "so Luke give me a fair deal on both cars." well it's depends on the method of payment" Luke admitted. Cash! Jah'me quickly stated.

Rob is going to go crazy when he see this bitch, "phew! Luke walked Jah'me around to his office, so they could talk on a more personal level, Jah'me I'm quite flattered that you want to buy two of my most expensive cars, but before I sell them to you, May I ask where your employed?"

I'm "self employed! Jah'me answered. Look I sell a lot of cars to young "self-employed men like yourself, and they don't even get to drive them for a month before the "Fed's take them away. I'd hate to see that happen to you." I'm a "multimillionaire so I'm not pressed for no cash, I just think you deserve to have something nice and to be able to keep it at the same time. Luke added. So what you got a job for me? Jah'me asked.

"No Luke said. " I have an investment for you. I just opened a club in DC called lovely nights. We can joint venture and go half. The club averages "fifty grand a night and that's just the door. It's open seven days a week and holds "five hundred at maximum capacity.

"so how much you want? Jah'me asked. At least half a "million! I don't have that now! Jah'me admitted.

"You will if you don't buy those cars! Luke responded. Look since you like the cars so much give me a "hundred "grand and I'm going to write up the contract and hold them for you, and when your money get right their both yours! They shook on it and he promised to get back with Luke at a later time.

Just then he received the call from Dave, telling him that the package was going to be at the soap and suds car wash on maple Rd, and to purchase the deluxe gold package, and once you enter the wash, beep your horn twice turn your lights on and pop your trunk, and once you hear a knock on the trunk that means the transaction is complete.

Kandy took off headed towards the drop spot! Jah'me was excited he couldn't even imagine having a "hundred brick's, I still can't believe this shit happening he said to Kandy. It's well deserved baby you work hard to make sure your whole crew eat, it's only right that the blessing returns back to you, she replied.

Once the arrived at the pick up they followed all instructions. Jah'me noticed two men in yellow rain coats, loading his trunk. And when they were finished they knocked on the trunk twice, Jah'me immediately told Kandy to pulled off!

Was this the luckiest day of his life? Or was it finally his time to shine? Jah'me thought to himself, how rare it was to meet two connects in one day.

Back at the hotel they popped the trunk and noticed five duffle bags, they quickly grabbed them and headed towards their room!

"so you can't tell me if she's been released? Michelle asked the woman on the other end of the phone. No ma'am! We are not allowed to disclose that information."

That's crazy! Michelle said "what if I was a victim of a crime she committed? Sorry ma'am! The operator replied.

Well thanks for nothing bitch! She pulled up her face book and twitter page's, telling herself that somebody knows something about that bitch!!!

"Damn a hundred bricks exactly! It's really one

hundred and fifty after we cut it up! And we breaking these bitches down! And shipping some to the Prison's where we going to triple our profit, That's the only way we going to see the come up Cuzzo said.

And I agree Jah'me replied, especially when you talking bout getting that Bentley coupe nigga!

PJ said Westville had been doing numbers but Lakeville was the money pot! PJ said after talking to his corrections officers he had on payroll, Their all ready to go! Bet Jah'me said giving him the go ahead to get the ball rolling.

Kandy sat back and observed how happy they were, it was like brothers unwrapping Christmas gifts on Christmas Eve! she was happy, she could come through for Jah'me and the NFL crew. she sat back and quietly played her position as she always did.

Now that Jah'me was officially a brick holder, he decided to move his whole team into one big house. He called Rob and had him to find a estate on private property, somewhere out VA , Beach.

Back at the condo the NFL crew all sat and listened to Jah'me as he explained how things were going to change.

When I went to DC! He began to explain. I met two connects, One was Kandy's people's Donte a straight forward honest man who dealt with principal. He fronted me these bricks and y'all know how much I hate working for anyone!

Why you didn't just buy joints PJ added. That's what I went to do "dick head! I think he see the potential, and wants to keep me in his pockets. But I'm cool with it for now. So what we going to do is, break this work down, pay him at least two more times and we gone! That's the plan so we can't fuck up in no way! Every single "dollar counts. Y'all with me? "Jah'me asked. They all shook their heads in agreement.

"As far as my second connect, his name is Luke. Another "Multimillionaire nigga! He wants to go into a joint venture investment he owns a club out in DC called lovely Nights. The club holds five hundred and averages almost hundred-grand a night. y'all can do the math yourselves. That's a lot of dead slave masters Cuzzo added laughing.

" It's our time to shine, but don't let this shit go to y'all head's. Stay loyal, and humble, Play with principal and always be fair. You will never get anywhere trying to get over on people. You feel me? Kandy is apart of our family now, so treat her accordingly. I know this situation seem a little awkward, but we can fuck any bitch we want, she N.F.L Now!   Jah'me concluded.

I bet my life Jah' still gone be hitting that PJ told Cuzzo. I would too if she was on my din-a-ling the way she on his. PJ stood up laughing at Cuzzo's crazy ass.

Rob pulled up to the beautiful baby mansion and was greeted by Kelly, a local realtor who specializes in luxury estate's. She and Rob had been talking on the phone for the past couple of mornings, and today was the open house. " Hello Rob? She inquisitively greeted.

" Yes! I'm Rob " he responded. I'm Kelly the one you spoke with on the phone. " Damn, Kelly you're very beautiful! He complimented. Kelly looked Brazilian, and had on thee tightest dress and come "fuck me heels, as she strutted through the estate.

" Rob this estate is fully furnished, we have the movie theater over to the right, it seats twelve comfortably. And over her is the gym equipped with everything you can imagine, and right down the hall, just to the right is the indoor swimming pool. I can smell the chlorine. Do you swim Kelly? " Yes! I try to go swimming at least once a week. Ok I will keep note of that he replied back!

Upstairs we have six bedrooms. But the master

bedroom is to die for." As they entered Rob couldn't believe his eyes. This room had a fully stocked bar, a Jacuzzi, a beautiful fire place and an entire kitchen.

" Damn! this might be too much! He added. I think you can handle it Kelly said trying to secure her sale. " How much he asked? It's been on the market six months, It was originally going for 2.3 but due to Covid -19 the housing market is at it's lowest. So your getting it today for an estimated 1.2 million. Not bad at all and what you get in commission? Twenty thousand she replied back smiling.

Rob laid back on the bed, this is nice! " you can't lay in the bed. Why not he replied back! Because it's not yours yet!

He could tell she was really feeling him too. " come sit with me Kelly you had me walking around this big as estate for over an hour. Relax beautiful, she sat beside him as he began to caress her legs and breast. You must be buying this house? She coaxes. You must be going to bend that ass over. Rob replied back.

For that commission hell the fuck yeah! She said.

She stopped and immediately pulled out the contract. " what's that? " Rob asked laughing.

Business before pleasure! She said passing him her ink pen. He skimmed the contract making sure the numbers were what Kelly told him they were once he spotted 1.2 million he signed.

As soon as he looked up Kelly was standing azz naked! Congratulations you have a beautiful home she said excited for the sale.

Rob stood up and dropped his pants and said for "twenty grand I sure hope you can eat a "dick up! She smiled and say's, I'm certainly going to try.

"Cuzzo had been partying at Blakey's night club located in the Chesapeake section of the city. He and a few friends took pictures and brought bottles in the V.I.P. Cuzzo was feeling himself his money was right and his team was eating.

After drinking champagne all night, he decided to buy a couple shots of Hennessy before the bar closed for the night. After making a couple calls to get him some ass, he left the club headed Up-Town to pick up one of his late night creeps freaky Trina. He would always take the back streets at night because the police were too serious in Chesapeake, and on top of that he was riding dirty.

Suddenly he was cut off by a driver coming at him head on, he swerved to get out of the on coming cars way and "crashed into a light pole, and was knocked out unconscious. When he came too! He was in the hospital handcuffs to the bed with an officer guarding his door. A nurse walked in to check on him. How long have I been here miss?

" Five hours she replied. What happened to me? You were in a car wreck, I overheard the police saying you were charged with reckless driving and D.U.I., but I guess you don't remember anything! You kids are going to learn one day. she said existing out of his room. "The fuck up" your old ugly flat booty ass!!! Cuzzo said under his breath. He pulled the rail trying to break the hand cuff. He couldn't go to jail, fuck no!! shit was going to good the team was just starting to eat. Ten minutes later she returned with a detective advising him that he would be released into their custody. He sat their and shook his head, with one thing on his mind. Jah'mes going to be pissed the fuck off!!

Luke was proud that Jah'me decided to invest his money. See Jah'me now you can drive anything you want to drive and them cracker's can't take it from you. You're an official business investor! With a partnership that generates a revenue of over two million dollars a year.

You can buy a shuttle and fly that bitch into space legally, with a kiss my black ass bumper sticker!

When your legal. Luke said laughing...

" Man I appreciate the love Luke but why me ace? Jah'me inquired.

Jah'me I saw the old me in you, when you drove up to my lot. I also noticed that you we're well respected by the Kidd Cuzzo, he just kept saying, my Boss will buy me this shit! It's light! the money ain't nothing.

I thought he was tripping out! but when you arrived, I was like hell no! Because you looked so young, but the aura and energy you brought with you, told me that you were the real deal! Now if we can get you out of them damn streets. Luke joked.

Jah'me laughed and said Luke that's all I know Nephew!

Kandy was back at the condo, doing her hair when Jah'me walked up and surprised her with her diamond necklace Happy birthday Kandy! "Aahh! It's beautiful! You remembered my birthday? She asked.

Of course. I could never forget such a important day, even though Donte reminded him Get dressed you, me, and the crew going to celebrate at Captain George's. Kandy was ass naked and he didn't even touch her.

"Daddy she called. "Yeah what's good? Can you and I go to dinner without the crew? I already told them an hour ago they been ready, we just waiting on you, His response causes her to cry. What's wrong he immediately asked?

I love you and you don't love me! Kandy yelled! You know I care about you, but it's different, the way we met just keep playing back in my mind, and how the crew ran a train on you, I lost that love, but without a doubt, I care about you more than you will ever know.

 But I want us to have more Daddy! Kandy said." we do! He said, you have my respect something you didn't have at first, maybe in due time things will work it self out, just continue to hold it down and keep it a band and we will always be good. She watched him exist the room thinking to herself that she'd missed another opportunity to tell him the truth!!

Jah'me received a call that Cuzzo was locked up in the Chesapeake jail for a D.U.I he tossed the burner phone over the Berkeley bridge, after finding out that, he didn't even have a fucking bond.

Luke called and said, the grand opening for the club was Saturday and he wanted Jah'me and his crew to show up. He begin to name some of the elite, that would be in attendance, Jah'me assured him that they would be their.

Jah'me pulled up at the mansion and couldn't believe his eyes, this house is crazy! Rob then bumped his damn head, he said standing in the brand new immaculate drive way.

How much was this house Rob? 1.1million ace! But it's worth it he was trying not to get the third degree. So far so good Jah'me said under his breath, this a long ways from section eight ace! Once inside everyone yelled welcome home and began popping bottles.

This is our house we earned this, but we got to work even harder to keep it Jah'me said. But with hard work and dedication, each one of you will have your own mansion, this is just the beginning of a Domino effect!

Tray's, Tray's, the C/O yelled! What the fuck is that, Cuzzo asked his cellie. That's just the police telling us it's chow Time! What the fuck is this shit they serving us anyways, Cuzzo asked pushing the tray away. " that's called shit on a shingle! Looks like it too, you can have it Cuzzo said baling his face up.

Man you haven't eaten in two days, you got to eat something, I know how it is coming off the streets

eating real food compared to this processed shit".
I'm good nephew, I'll survive off of bread and
orange juice!! No disrespect but that shit stink.

 Tell that to my stomach, he not trying to hear that!
His cellie said sprinkling salt and pepper on
Cuzzo's tray.

This is a collect call from .....Cuzzo, an inmate at
the Chesapeake city jail. To accept the charges
press one. Kandy immediately answered. "Boy I'm
going to kill you! What the hell you doing driving
drunk? Your ass don't even have a bond yet! When
is your court date?

In two weeks! Cuzzo answered. Jah'me is pissed
at you, he said you know better. Where's the
Lexus?" It's in the pound. That's why I'm calling
you, I need you to go and get it before they search
it and find the stash box. "Ok I got you! Anything
else? "yeah I need some money on my books, this
food is unbearable!" ok how much? Five bills
should set me straight for now! Cuzzo replied.

"Ok I'll go get the car, then I will JPay you the
money, stay strong and keep your head up boy!
"you already know it's N.F.L for life. For life she
repeated and hung up.

Later that night, two black Cadillac trucks pulled in
front of the club. Jah'me and his crew had finally

arrived. Everybody in line continue to guestimate who they could be.

Suddenly Luke and several security workers existed the club. welcome to your establishment, as you can see, we have a good crowd waiting to get in, this is only half of them, the line continues to wrap around the block. I know we saw it as we were pulling in Jah'me replied.

It's twelve o clock so everyone must pay twenty five dollars to enter Luke assured him. Now that's what I call money! Jah'me said looking around the immaculate establishment, once in the VIP section, they quickly recognize the celebrity presence, from rappers, basketball ball stars, and models, were all in attendance.

Cuzzo couldn't believe it when he noticed his favorite porn stars, Diamond and Ms. Phat booty! Sitting directly across from them. Wing and PJ noticed them as well and they proceed to approach them. Jah'me laughed at his crew knowing them, he knew that by the end of the night, with PJ talking, somebody's panties were coming off!

Dave was Donte's lieutenant, he and Donte had been friends since college, they both played football and we're athletic standouts. Dave played middle line backer and Donte played quarterback. They lived and rented an apartment together on campus, where they sold weed and molly to make ends meet, but Donte never sold anything. He would always score and then expect Dave to off the package.

After reviewing recruitment letters from the New Orleans Saints, Tampa Bay buccaneers, and LA Rams. Dave decided to fall back from selling drugs because he didn't want to Jeopardize his NFL career. But Donte wanted him to off the last of what was left, to secure the next months rent.

And once again Dave went back on his word, he felt like a flunkie at times. while Donte was running around like a super star. He was at spot cooking up and selling work.

One Saturday Evening he was bagging up molly, when the front door came crashing down! Dave was arrested and charged with P.W.I.D. he was discharged from school and was sentenced to a year in jail. During that year he watched his best friend get the draft to the NFL.

Dave placed all the blame on Donte for him not being in the NFL. To him he's back to being a flunkie, just on a higher level. He knew one day he would get his get back! But for now he still had a job to do.

Nobody at the mansion liked Dave he was bitter and kept an attitude. Dee didn't even rock with him because of his energy!

He knew in his heart that he had something to do with Dave's incarceration. So when Dave was released from jail, he was the first to greet him with a Bentley coupe and three million dollars.

Dave happily took the money and brought him a luxury condo in Washington, DC where he tried to open a couple of businesses that failed along with his stock and Realastate investments.

He was on a downward spiral to being broke again! He took his last hundred grand and called Spanish Juan.

Spanish Juan charged him, thirty- five a brick.

After Dave told Donte, he called one of his connections and a large shipment was delivered the three days later. He told Dave if your going to sell drugs, you might as well do it right and go all out! And once again Dave found himself being Donte's flunkie...

The club turned out to be a success, Jah'me loved the atmosphere, it had a grown and sexy vibe to it. Club lovely was lit" the females was like no other they had seen before. It's like whenever the DJ played any go-go music, the women became demonly possessed! one song could play for thirty minutes or longer. They would come out of their clothes and everything! The crew learned quickly how freaky them DC bitches could get!

Ms. Phat- Phat and Diamond was drunk as hell, they began sucking the crew off in the VIP. PJ talked them into going to the mansion and having a sex party. Jah'me and Kandy stayed back took pictures and met the rest of the staff. Luke approach Jah'me passing him his first thirty thousand dollar check.

I know you have a lot going on Jah'me I just ask if you can show up to the club once a week, so people will know who you are! Luke suggested.

" I like to play the background Luke! With the money your going to be making, your going to need to be known, if not your going to be getting watched anyways my friend! Luke replied.

Four hour's later,,,, Back at the mansion. Jah'me pulled up and noticed his driveway full of luxury cars, you could hear the music outside. Kandy and Jah'me entered and walked in to a live orgy. The crew had Diamond folded up on the couch like a pretzel. While PJ had Phat-Phat all to himself.

51

Kandy grabbed Jah'me by the hand and walked him upstairs to the master bedroom and locked the door, she wanted him all to herself.

Detective Cobb's and Agent Vick, were assigned to the case. They were informed that Marcus Williams (Cuzzo) had a conversation on the global TEL phone system, telling the receiver of the call to go and retrieve drugs from his stash box. The Agents confiscated the Lexus, and it's being held pending further investigation...

The next morning Jah'me woke up drained, he decided to go downstairs to get a glass of orange juice. when he noticed Diamond was sitting in the Jacuzzi by herself. What's good diamond? Nothing much just trying to relax , we acted up last night! hell yeah he replied back getting in to join her.

 This house is gorgeous. Thanks I just purchased it a week ago! Well what a way to break it in, Diamond joked. Yeah we definitely broke this bitch in. It's always fun whenever your around a mature group of people. How old are you by the way Jah'me? Twenty he replied. How about you Diamond what's your real name? Natasha Reed and I'm twenty-nine. Do you make good money doing porn? He inquired.

Yeah! I do now! At first I was getting jerked around but that's the business. You have to go the independent route, I shoot and produce all of my scenes. That's why I get paid now!

That's some real boss shit! Natasha! I fucked with you the long way! Definitely Can't knock the Hussle! He encouraged.

"I like you Jah'me you cool as shit. I want to invite you to my convention it's a full week. You get to meet all of your favorite starlets. I already did he said with a wink. But without a doubt I accept your invite, just make sure I'm on the list. VIP baby she replied.

Dave was whack as hell and Jah'me hated dealing with him. He was never on time and he didn't know how to handle business properly. On his last shipment Dave charged Jah'me twenty five a bird,(those numbers were not even the type of numbers Donte would have charge me) he thought to himself. Let me off the rest of this work and I'm going to get back with you Dave, that number a little high right now!

That's the price take it or leave it! Dave screamed through the phone. First and for most lower that frequency big fella we not doing , no back and fourth shit, it's going to be, what's it's going to be gangster!!! Like I said I'm going to get back with you. Jah'me hung up, As the phone went silent in Dave's ear.

"Williams, Williams! You have a visit the c/o yelled! That's one of my homies coming through to show some love ya digg! Cuzzo told told his cellmate.

Cuzzo walked to the visitation room only to be redirect to the interview room. He sat for a moment, before two white men entered flashing their badges.

I'm agent Vick and this is agent Cobb's, your case has been deemed federal.

Back at the Mansion the crew all sat back and discussed Cuzzo's case. When is his court date? Jah'me asked. Sometime next month, the clerk told me Kandy said. That nigga stupid as hell! I been told his azz to stop fucking driving without his L'S. He so fucking Gas happy.

Wing entered the room shaking his head, well I just got off the phone with Tellaferra and he said Cuzzo case went federal. Federal! What the fuck you mean? I know this boy wasn't driving dirty, that's not even our style, and this Federal shit ain't sitting good with me.

Anybody else then done some dumb shit I need to

know about he questioned? They all shook their heads no, as Jah'me walked out of the room. Once again Kandy missed a golden opportunity to come clean....

Mr. Williams we know about the half of brick of Cocaine and the gun you had in your car. What car and what gun Cuzzo asked? Looking confused. The car that had the AK-47 with your finger prints all over it! Cuzzo continued playing dumb.

Agent Vick slammed the tape recorder on the table, we have your stupid black ass on tape. Listen! After listening to the tape agent Vick asked if he was ready to corporate or play hard? Do you know the Fed's have a 99.8 percent conviction rate?

I'm not even going to lie phew, that ain't even me talking. Somebody set me up! Cuzzo stated. it's only two types of prisoner's in the Fed's, agent Vick said, the ones that snitched and the ones who wished they did, Don't be a fool, all the evidence points towards you. Would you like a cigarette? "Hell yeah! Cuzzo replied.

Would you like anything else? My partner here agent Cobbs will make sure your taken good care of. Just relax and talk to us, I promise we're only here to help you, were not your enemies. "Man I'm hungry! Cuzzo stated. "what would you like to eat agent Vick asked?

"A double whopper cut in half with cheese from Burger King, McDonald's fries, an apple pie. You can top it off with a rallies banana milkshake. "That's a lot of running around to different restaurants, if we provide you this food will you cooperate? Hell yeah Cuzzo said.

The agent left out leaving handcuffed to the table with a pack of Newport's and a book of matches, he stuffed six Newport's in his sock to take back to the jail.

The agents walked in a hour later with the food. They sat and watches him devour everything like he hadn't eaten in weeks. After drinking the milk shake Cuzzo let out a loud burp!

"Now that's what the fuck I'm talking about Cuzzo said lighting up a Newport laughing.

Agent Vick asked what was so funny? Man I'm not telling y'all crackers shit, take me back to the jail.

You little bitch! I'm going to make sure your ass get forty-years and get shipped to New Mexico far from your ugly ass mother!

"Fuck you! Cuzzo yelled. N.F.L. for life "

What the hell does that mean? Agent Cobbs asked,

agent Vick!

"National football league, dumb asses , go Saints......!

Kandy was living the good life. She had her own room at the mansion and could come and go as he please, Jah'me even up graded her from being his driver to being his accountant. She kept the bills paid and made sure the payroll was done. And For her promotion Jah'me brought her a hot pink Lexus coupe with, white leather bucket seats and he raised her pay to twenty- grand a month.

That's the type of money she needed as much as she loved to shop. just recently, she heard through PJ that Kim her best friend was coming home, and she wanted nothing more than to take her out on a hair, nails, spa, and shopping spree. That's was her girl since the sandbox.

Back UP-Town, Kandy immediately noticed "Mrs. Brenda sitting on her porch, hello Ms. Brenda how you been, I'm Kandy" Kim's best friend! "oh lord girl, I know who you are. Kandy you look so different! I know I've gained a little weight Ms. Brenda! Kandy admitted. A little! Ms. Brenda joked. I hardly noticed you girl, but you look good. Kim ass in their sleep, go on in and wake her up! She's going to be happy as hell to see you.

Kandy's heart was racing the last time she saw Kim they both jumped Kesha from Roberts park. As soon as The six foot, two hundred thirty pound knock out queen exited the shower, Kim pulled a pillow case over her head and Kandy wailed on her until she saw blood.

Kesha was undefeated in the jail, but Kandy and Kim had her number that day, and that was the last time, they she saw one another until now!

The bedroom still looked the same, Kandy noticed several pictures, of the two of them still hanging on the wall. She began to cry. Kim felt someone's presence in the room and turned over to see her best friend, she screamed Kandy!!!!

Rob and Kelly kept in contact on the regular and had plans on getting together for a nice romantic candle light dinner. Since the crew were all going to California, he decided he would house sit.

Kelly always wondered what Rob did for a living, Rob told her several times that he played over seas. But his aura felt like drug dealer all day. "

well hopefully we can hook up next week, I miss you! Kelly said. Same here! Replied Rob. What you got on under that dress girl? Some pink silk boy shorts. Damn I know you bussing out them draws too!!

"Yep ass just shaking , want to hear me smack it? Kelly teased. Hell yeah Damn baby, I can't wait to hit that. Me either! Kelly replied. I have to get some rest I have a busy day tomorrow. Well Goodnight sweetheart. Rob hung the phone up thinking to himself, that's definitely wifey all day.

Before Cuzzo went back to his cell he was escorted to booking, where his picture and finger prints were taken again, but this time he was registering as a federal inmate.

Back at the mansion, Kandy and Jah'me was relaxing in his double king size bed watching celebrity homes. Damn Ray J! I would of thought you had a bigger spot than that nephew! At least two thousand square feet or better, that nigga living in a shoe box, he told Kandy as she laid their tripping off of him.

You mighty quiet today, you have something on your mind you want to talk about? No I'm good baby she replied back in her soft voice.

 It's a building vacancy in Janaf shopping center, I'm going to put a bid on it, if I win it, I plan on opening up a saloon. For real bae? Yeah and we going to call it, Kandy's unisex hair and nails.....

Damn baby you doing your thing Kandy said. Like Jeezy said the world is yours and everything in it!

you just got to want it, the harvest is plentiful Kandy it's enough money out here for everyone who really want it.

His phone started to ring. It was Cuzzo's lawyer. " I just left the jail Jah'me, I didn't get a chance to talk to Cuzzo, but I did pull his case file and to my knowledge his case has gone federal!"

"What the fuck? Jah'me yelled. I'm going to kill that nigga!

Calm down Jah'me, killing him will not make the situation better, I'm going to see what I can do. I will give you a call back by next week."

Jah'me walked into the trap spot they operated out of Virginia, Beach. It didn't look nothing like, the trap spots they were used to in Norfolk. This was a town house in a quiet neighborhood.

 It was the safest place for them to cook and bag up work. What's good? Jah'me greeted the crew. Shit PJ said weighing four and a half on the scale. Jah'me sat on the couch beside wing, who was counting money from out of the trash bag, Jah'me grabbed a hand full and started counting with him What happened to the money counter? Jah'me asked.

"Its jammed! PJ yelled from the kitchen. Damn!

Somebody call Kandy and tell her to buy another money counter and bring her ass over here to help count this money, she know it's count money Monday."

Speaking of Kandy . Remember when the whole crew took flicks at club love, and I told you I went to Booker t with the camera man? He told me he knew Kandy from back in the day, and that she just came home from doing a five year bid, in the Fed's for snitching!

Why you just telling me this Rob? He asked. Because I know you only go with facts, and not what a nigga say, So I had a inside source look her up.

 Her name is Rachel and she went to Booker T . Rob then opened a year book and their was without a doubt Kandy! Rob called her phone three times followed by Jah'me calls only to get no answer.

" That's bitch police! Jah'me said kicking' the flat screen to the floor and storming out.

Kandy and Kim had been chilling, spending money and catching up on old times. She left the phone in her car to charge. When she returned she noticed several missed calls from Rob and Jah'me. What the hell is going on...

"Damn girl this Lexus is dope how much you pay a month? This paid for Kandy boasted. Must be nice! Kim replied. "So who's the rich nigga you fucking. And does he have a rich friend?

"Yeah! They all have money, if I was to hook you up, it would be with Rob. He's your type laid back handsome and hung like a horse! Kandy informed.

you fucked him to? Kim asked? Yeah I fucked them all!! "So you like their whore? I guess you could have said that At first. But now I'm apart of the crew. And I'm only fucking my man, the B.O.S.S.! You feel me?

They both burst out laughing, because Kandy didn't even have to tell Kim that, she knew Kandy and the Kandy she'd always known was only attracted to Bosses!!!

Thank you so much for the shopping spree! Friend" you're the best Kim said opening the car door.

Kandy popped the trunk so she could retrieve her bags. Here is five bands it should hold you for now. Hell yeah Kim shouted! Now you don't have to ask nobody for shit! Thanks Bestie, but I'm Grateful for the shopping spree! You don't have to give me any Money.

I'd rather give it to you then to buy a bag! Thanks girl. You welcome. Give Mrs. Brenda a couple of hundred for me! and call me tomorrow morning, so we can find you an apartment, you can't be living out the projects your whole damn life, she said laughing while pulling off. Kandy felt good, being able to help Kim get back on her feet, that was her A1 since day one.

Her phone began to ring it was Rob.

"Hello Kandy!! Yeah! What's wrong Rob? A whole lot. First and foremost why you never told us that you just came home from prison. And that your originally from Up-Town? Kandy almost dropped her phone. Who told you that? She asked.

Kandy you need to come clean. Jah'me would kill me if he found out that I'm even talking to you right now, he knows everything, and you need to tell him. You been lying, I don't know your reason but I hope its justified.

I like you a lot Kandy but I love my niggas more!! whatever the case hopefully we can get pass it and move forward, but you know, I don't have the final say.

Just let him cool off and come home a little later. I'll talk to him, he has a lot on his plate right now! The plug Dave tripping on the numbers. Cuzzo's case then went Federal, and now this. He's dealing whit a lot, But I'm out remember just be honest because he knows.....

Kandy hung up scared and confused she rolled a blunt and sat in McDonald's parking thinking and praying.

Jah'me had gotten real popular in the night club scene, he met and mingled with lots of athletes and celebrities, he just recently just exchanged numbers with young Jeezy, after he performed at his club on labor day weekend, along with his favorite quarter back and his homie.

Just a month ago, I was a regular nigga Luke! Jah'me said. Luke looked at him and said, when your making millions of Dollars, your going to be amongst the elite! And as far as you being regular, I haven't met a man under twenty-five yet to pull up on my lot wanting to purchase my two most expensive cars. Regular niggas dream of doing the shit you do on the regular, my friend like assured him.

Kandy called Rob's phone, to see if it was a good time to come home. He told her that Jah'me was making his out of town run and wouldn't be back until around 1am. And that they would get everything out and on the table, and hopefully

64

handled like adults. She told Rob that was scared but knew and understood as their phones disconnected.

Cuzzo's court date was in two days. He was called for a visit, when he arrived he noticed that it was Kandy. What's up girl!

Hey" Cuzzo! you doing alright?" she asked. Yeah I'm maintaining. why you looking sad, I know you and something ain't right. It's a lot Cuzzo.. Kandy began, but how did the Fed's pick up your case? They said that they have a recording of me talking to a female over the phone about drugs in my Lexus.

Damn Cuzzo we knew better! She stated. Yeah but they don't know Shit! I did just put the car in my girlfriend name a month ago, they tried to say the car was in my name. I knew they was lying too! He said laughing. I just might walk Monday Kandy. Well I hope so she added. What Jah'me and the crew doing? He asked.

He is upset with me at the moment, because I lied about something! She admitted. "Oh that's nothing, I lie all the time. Kandy started laughing. You're family though. My situation is very serious and I'm scared as fuck Cuzzo!

Kandy arrived back at the mansion around three

thirty in the morning, she noticed Jah'mes Benz parked, along side of Rob's BMW . Which made her feel a little better.

She existed her car in her dress that showed her curvaceous body, she was definitely ready for a photo shoot. She entered the estate through the game room. She could smell the weed and scented candle aroma, as she walked through the house. Trey songs was singing through the Bose house speakers.

Her thoughts we're interrupted when she heard a female voice giggling, she walked up and saw Jah'me getting head from a Spanish bombshell, her feelings were all the way hurt, but she knew the count!! As soon as he noticed Kandy, he grabbed his gun and hurry towards her..

Who the fuck are you? If you lie! I swear on my dead brother Im going to kill your ass right now!

Im from Up-Town and I just came home from doing a five year stretch! I didn't tell you because I've been labeled a snitch!! Who you tell on Kandy bitch!! I told on Trey because he left me for dead when I was the one who took the fall for him, but the streets were saying I told on his crew, Jack, killer, and Daz!

I know all of them Rob said, that nigga Daz was a

snake for real.

I can't trust you and if it's no trust it's no loyalty. I felt something wasn't right with you, and I kept asking you, if it was something you needed to tell me! You got to go! You can have everything you got from me, but leave my property ASAP, and never show your face around here again, Jah'me exited the room as fast as he came.

Kandy felt like her world has just come to an end, and she'd lost the man she truly loved, she sat in the driveway and cried. Her phone ringed and she noticed that it was Jah'me, Hello"? She said. "Bitch your on private property, leave before I start shooting, and this is my final warning! He said sounding cold hearted and serious. Kandy quickly pulled off headed anywhere the road took her.

The judge dismissed all of the charges on Cuzzo, since the car wasn't in his name and the drugs weren't in his possession, he was sentenced to time served for the DWI and reckless driving. Three hours later Cuzzo walked out of Chesapeake jail a free man. The first person he called was Rob, what's up? This Cuzzo! I beat my case come pick me up bro!

"we out of town and won't be back until Friday, until then find a spot and lay low! You need some bread Rob asked? I'm good for now I still got the money I had left on my books. I'm going to my baby mom's spot until you all get back. Bet Rob said hanging up . Jah'me was sitting beside Rob the entire call.

"He out Jah'me asked?

"yeah! Rob replied back. Change everybody's numbers, he either being watched by them people or he "snitching!! I don't have him snitching, either way we need to stay far away from Cuzzo! We doing to much and can't afford no slip ups! I got you Jah' I'm on top of it!

"Cuzzo's baby mother lived out "Tidewater park. she had four hard headed boy's and one girl. He hated to go their but he had no choice, when he entered the house he immediately hugged his baby mother and daughter. Agent Vick was sitting in his car parked across the street. "Fed's taking pictures….

Luke called Jah'mes phone, what the Business is he greeted? "same ole shit Luke replied.

How you and the crew holding up? He and Luke had gotten tighter over the months and their friendship turned into a brother hood. Luke was the brother he never had, he told Luke about Kandy and Cuzzo, Luke advise him to fall back! but to stay on point.

 I have these two luxury cars holding up space when do you plan on picking them up? Luke asked. "The Bentley and Phantom, been paid for, I can have my workers do the paperwork and put the thirty's on them both. When should they be expecting you? Give me five hours ace I'm on my way!

"Be careful and remember these cars put you in a while different class. So stay humble, and always remember, that real hustlers move in silence.

You think Im ready for them whips Luke? You have the income to vouch for you, I know you can handle it. Remember you only live once! Luke coxed. Facts Jah'me replied back, he hung up and called Rob with the exciting news! they had a couple spaceships to pick up!

Back at the federal building located on Brambleton Ave in the Downtown section of Norfolk, VA. The agents were having a debriefing on their recent case. Agent Cobbs and Agent Vick were talking to at least twenty different DEA taskforce agents!

"Our target here is "Marcus Williams knowned as "Cuzzo. He is knowned to frequent the Downtown Norfolk area, our Intel tell us that he runs with a group of drug dealers, that's been under the radar and have been pulling in millions in drug profits.

 This kid "Marcus Williams AKA Cuzzo is only nineteen and has had over eight luxury vehicles, our records show, he recently just crashed a 2021 Lexus last week! We know the game of putting the properties in other people's name. He is getting major money and I know he is just the small fish, that can lead us to the bigger one's.

He is knowned to run with this crew. "A picture of Rob, PJ, Wing, Cuzzo, Kandy, and Jah'me appeared on the screen.

This man to the right (Jah'me) we can't say he is apart of this crew, we do know he is part owner of the club they were in this Saturday night. So maybe they just wanted to take a picture with the owner some type of flex if you get my drift.

 We know the guy next to him name is "PJ, he is a knowned drug dealer, our records show he did a five years in prison for a shooting. The guy next to him is "Rob he is the "Lieutenant. How do you know he is involved in the drug market one agent asked? Looking at his record, he is clean cut and works at a "barber shop! I can have agent Shantez elaborate further.

A pretty Spanish Agent walked up from the back of the room, to the front podium. Good evening ladies and gentlemen, my name is Kelly Shantez and I'm the agent investigation this case..

After checking his voice mail Jah'me realized, the convention was coming up. Diamond had left at least five messages, he called back and she answered on the second ring, " boy where have you been, I've been doing my best to reserve you V.I.P. spot" she said sounding excited. It jumps off Saturday so are you available? What you think diamond, me and the crew will be their. How many you bringing? "she asked. "Four! Rob, PJ, and Dee money! He informed." Dee money the football star She asked gleefully. "yeah that's my guy, we kick it whenever he comes to my club!"

"Well good! She said. Ms. Phat Phat told me to tell you hello and that she will see you at the convention".

Rob walked in and asked Jah'me who he was talking to, hoping he would say Kandy. He missed having her around the house just didn't seem the same.

That was Diamond! She wanted to know if we were still coming to the convention".

Count me out! got something planned this weekend. Man these are porn bitches you ok my nigga! Yeah I know but I got shit lined up already

Jah'!

What you can do is check up on Cuzzo. Tell him to fall back, for a couple of months, we will holler back at him, make sure he knows not try and contact us in any way. Take him some changed so he can maintain too!

Cuzzo was back out "Tidewater park smoking weed while playing the game, he tried to call in a chicken dinner meal from Feather and Fin, and noticed his phone had been clipped!

"What the fuck? "He yelled! He knew that they all had the same group plan. If my phone off then that means that theirs is too. He dialed Rob's number from his baby mother's phone, only to be told it was disconnected, he did the same with the rest of the crew and received the same message.

"Miska Cuzzo? " the snotty nose little boy said. "can I have some money?

"I ain't your daddy nigga, go steal from the store like I had too, He replied back to the child. Suddenly A loud knock was at the door." Who is it ? "Cuzzo asked.

Big bro! What's Poppin bro? That five Rob replied back. I miss y'all where everybody at? " They cooling! Rob said. Look Jah'me sent me to tell you that he love you, but you hott right now nephew! He changed everybody's number.

How the fuck I'm hott " I beat my case, bro! "Cuzzo use your head, whenever the "Fed's pick you up, the majority of the time, they've got a case. Just lay low for a couple of months. Here is sixty thousand in cash.

Cuzzo tossed the money on the floor, man fuck that money. I want my brothers. I ain't no fucking snitch!!!. I told them "Fed's to kiss my black ass and I came home "phew", and this how y'all treat me? What happened to "NFL?

Rob pointed to the money on the ground, "you got that because you "N.F.L! And he walked away. He never noticed the black van across the street. "Fed's taking pictures.

Kelly had been a DEA agent for the past several years. Her grandfather, father, and brother were all agents as well. So it was in her blood line to be a cop. Her father was killed in a drug raid, by drug dealers in 1989. She will never forget that day, she vowed to join the force and bust as many drug dealers as she could on the east coast.

Throughout the years, she began to earn rank, as a result of her many successful drug raids, busting the small fish began to get boring. knowing, that's all drug kingpin's loved, luxury cars, and homes. She decided to get into the Realastate market, expecting a drug dealer will come along soon. she was only a realtor six months before she met Rob. A young black with loads of cash looking to buy a home. After doing her own investigations she realized that he was what she had been working for the last seven years, The Big Fish,,,,

Rob met Kelly at Ruby Tuesday's for dinner. It had been a long and stressful day running around then having to deal with the cuzzo situation. He was dressed business casual slacks and gators with his twenty caret flawless princess cut bracelet along with the Rolex watch that Jah'me gifted to him. Kelly also was dressed very sexy her hair was dark, long and curly, and it always looked wet .

"Hello beautiful! He said taking a seat at the table. So how was your day? Kelly was shocked that he had asked that. It had been many years and many dates since she heard that question from any man. " It was ok! She responded back, and yours. "Hectic but that come with the job sometimes. You smell wonderful is that Prada Candy? "Yes Kelly shockingly responded. I see you know your perfumes. "of course just like I know my women" ummm! What you know about me? She asked. I know your favorite color is green, you're a Scorpio, and you have on a Vera Wang dress, and Carol Bennett stilettos, I also know that you're very smart, visual, and your always aware of your surroundings".

" How did know that? She asked." Because I watched your body Language. My best friend is great at reading people and being around him makes me better at it as well, I love your lips can I taste them?

Kelly licked her lips and kisses Rob deeply with passion. She thought to herself that she had to stop before she got attached to this handsome man, but that burning desire in her said it was already too late!

"Lil baby's voice of the voice of the heroes blasted through the speakers of the phantom, as Jah'me burned the interstate up headed back to the "Seven Cities. He couldn't believe the looks he was receiving, when he and Wing stopped at the gas station, cars starting pulling in just to get a glimpse at who could be the potential star behind the wheel.

 The over crowding at the station cause the police to come and escorted them away. A group of teenagers in a ls 430 yelled out of their window, is y'all with cash money? Wing replied back we are cash money, and pulled off behind Jah'me. when they arrived back to the mansion that parked both cars in the driveway.

Jah'me you showed your ass this time bro! I originally got these cars for Rob and Cuzzo, but with all the attention that come with these cars I'm glad cuzzo ain't getting one. "So who's car is it now Jah'? "

Yours for now. Don't be wilding out Cuzz! Jah'me instructed wing! I won't my nigga that's my word! Wing said excitedly. That's the same shit cuzzo said. Jah'me shook his head laughing.

They walked into the mansion and shut the door, they never noticed the agents disguised as Cox cable workers taking pictures.

Hollywood was home to the movie stars and rich people. Jah'me rented a 2023 Maybach. Wing, PJ, and Dee money, were all in towe rolling down Rodeo Drive. Their go Eddie Murphy!" PJ rolled down the window. A Eddie, stop looking for boy's wit your gay ass! everyone started laughing.

They were welcomed to the convention center, by half naked women on the red carpet, wearing G-strings and see through tops.

Do you have tickets? the woman at the door asked

PJ. Jah'me exited the car with the rest of the crew and informed the lady that they were on the V.I.P. list.

She recognized Dee money and instantly allowed him to enter, when he told the lady that he was their with Jah'me, she allowed them all to enter. They had to have at least a million dollars worth of jewelry combined between the four of them.

Diamond spotted them and quickly ran over to greet them all . "Hello guys, I'm glad to see that you all made it here safe." I told you I would be here even though we scrambled in like eggs getting in.

My bad Jah'me, I left for five minutes and you pop -up, I apologize for that Jah'me. Make yourselves comfortable! Diamond said we're going to blow your minds this weekend, ain't nothing but half naked bitches all over this place..

The estate was finally quiet, Rob had the maids retire to their quarters for the remainder of the night, but before they left he had them place and light a hundred candles around his king size bed and Jacuzzi, rose petals and bottles of wine were chilled on ice I a bucket, the fire place was burning and Jah'mes favorite Gerald LeVert song was playing in the background.

"Yeah! That's nice! Rob said admiring the view from the hit tub. The door bell rang and he knew it was Kelly. She smiled and greeted him as soon as he opened the door. She had on a long trench coat covering her whole body

"Allow me to take your coat! Rob offered. As he took the coat she had a matching Victoria secret bra and panties set on. "when God made you, he took his time with all this thickness!

you so crazy! She replied as Rob guided her to the jacuzzi, this is really nice and romantic Rob".

Lets make a toast to a long lasting relationship. I see you got half a million in the driveway!" she said referring to the two luxury cars in the driveway.
" Oh they just a few toys, Something light. "Yeah whatever! She joked! "come here! I'm not going to bite! Rob said as he began to caress her face and hair.

Kelly was falling in love with a suspect and couldn't do anything about it, because Rob wasn't anything she had expected. He wasn't out Killing and committing crimes. He was a kind hearted Teddy bear who cared for her , and she couldn't do anything about it, she had fallen in love with a thug!

"Man that shit was crazy Dee money shouted from the front seat. Yeah I had a ball we definitely got to

78

do this again, they will never allow a convention like that in the Commonwealth! PJ joked.

At the red light at village and Rodeo Dr. Jah'me noticed an fleet of luxury cars. Directly beside him was a young man in a Lambo. Jah'me rolled his window down and asked "what he paid for the Lambo?

 at first Sight he wasn't going to answer. But he noticed the two-hundred thousand dollar George McDaniel's watch , and the twenty karat earrings that Jah'me sported in his left ear, and he knew he could afford one!

"A little piece of change!" the guy replied back. "Well it's nice! Jah'me replied.

Well look we headed over to the car wash over on village, if you want to test drive her, just follow me! "He then allowed Jah'me to cut into the entourage.

Dee money decided to stay in the car he didn't want all the attention, so the rest of the crew existed the car. What's happening I'm Jah'me! And this is my crew. "Im BK he told Jah'me. "Where you from? Jah'me asked. Originally from Brooklyn, by way of Houston, TX. And yourself BK asked?

"Im from Norfolk, VA ! Jah'me answered. I heard they do a lot of snitching down their! BK added.

That's everywhere ace! Jah'me replied back, that's why I keep the squares out of my circle and I only roll with family and money getters like myself. He said as Bk listened. By the way who's your favorite Quarter back, I have a few Joe Barrow, Russell Wilson, and the young boy out of VA making noise Dee money course he answered.

Jah'me called Dee money's phone and told him to roll down the window. As the window descended, Jah'me pointed to the car and Dee money nodded his head. "Aint that a bitch BK said excited" so what you pushing? Something light but looking for a blessing.

What you getting them for BK asked? Twenty-five, I can get the to you for fifteen five here's my number!

Back in the town cuzzo had brought another Lexus and had moved out beach. He brought a nice condo, he paid fourty-grand cash for. He still held a grudge about how Jah'me carried the situation. He didn't understand it, but fuck it, he had to move on. He called PJ several times meeting him Up-Town and scoring a bricks, for the low. PJ made him promise to never tell Jah'me that he was scoreing from him.

PJ did it because in his heart he knew Cuzzo

would never snitch, he loved the crew to much and they grew up together, and plus PJ wanted to see cuzzo win too.

Cuzzo was getting to the bag! And was now on his feet. He was sitting in the parking lot of Shop-N-Go when Kandy and Kim pulled in. Kim was the first to notice, the big luxury car. "Damn some nigga up here stunting hard in that 460". Kandy was looking good as always, the driver looked kind of fimilure, when she noticed the window roll down she screamed cuzzo! He existed the car and they hugged boy when did you get out?" she asked.

I been home a month! He informed her." How is Jah'me she asked? Man it's a long story I was about to ask you the same question. You looking good Kandy, ass all phat! That azz got phatter!" I've been and doing my squats, I need to loose some weight."

No the hell you don't! Cuzzo disagreed "you just right. I just brought a condo out the beach, come on over so we can catch up! "whats your address? She asked. I'll Tex it to you, meet me their in a hour. I'll be their she assured him.

The crew were all sitting around drinking and shooting pool. When Jah'me began to talk, Like Im saying fellas, we got to bring in more money this month.

We've been splurging hard, traveling first class, staying in the best hotel's and just living life. And That shit feels good! Wouldn't you agree? "he asked them. "Damn right I never envisioned us being like this bro! PJ replied. "so what you hustling for PJ? Jah'me asked.

To live my nigga, but I guess I was just existing then. I'm living now!

"It all comes with loyalty and hard work! Jah'me said passing Rob the blunt, we either in the game to get rich or it's a failed mission.

Did you all see the fleet of cars BK had? He said he owned each and every one of them, crazy right? We got to get our money up this month. So chill with the spending!

Jah'mes phone began to ring, it was Dave. What's good Dizzy!

"Good evening Mr. Jah'me! I'm sorry I can't relate to your hood ebonics, but I called to see when will you be picking up the package? "Where is it? It's in New Jersey Dave answered. Why is it in Jersey? Dover is hot as hell so is route one and seventeen and I'm super scared of that turnpike, I can't send my team on a dummy mission like that phew!

"Well phew! You either get it or forget it! Dave said with an attitude. Man you been tripping hard lately, for what I don't even know". I'm only going to talk about the shipment. Anything else is irrelevant and speaking of the shipment, you know you owe me a hundred dollars from the last shipment. I paid you a quarter million dollars and you tripping over a yard nigga! Don't ever disrespect me like that. You have three hours to pick up the shipment! David informed. And how is that even possible when I'm in Virginia dumb ass?"

Make a way Dave replied. You know what ? Jah'me began. "Fuck you and your shipment, you bitch ass nigga, and if you ever call my line again, I promise you I can get to DC in three hours and a half hours to kick your ass! David hung up.

"Damn phew! who was that? David bitch ass. I'm glad I don't owe him shit, I'm not dealing with him anymore. I just started networking with BK, he got them for the low. speaking of BK, I got to call him to let him know Im ready to invest.

Kandy pulled up to Cuzzo's house, she noticed he wasn't home yet, so she called his phone, he was pulling up in a couple of minutes. He pulled up happy as a kid on Christmas to see Kandy. They hugged and walked into his condo. Wow! This is nice cuzzo! She said looking around, he knew she loved reggae music, so he cranked up a Reggae gold ninty- seven.

Want a drink, Kandy? " he offered. " yeah why not she said grooving to the music, he passed her the blunt and she began to smoke.

After the third drink Kandy was drunk, cuzzo knew he was fucking Kandy tonight, she was something special, any nigga would wife her. But cuzzo wanted her for himself.

After an hour had passed, cuzzo decided to make his move, he walked behind her and palmed her ass," she turned around and said Boy I'm going to fuck the shit out of you. She turned around and dropped her dress to the floor.

Cuzzo was on the E-pill, weed, and Hennessy and had been fucking Kandy for almost two hours. So where do we go from here she asked? All the way to the top baby! He said knowing she was the one who could get him put on with her uncle Dee!

Agent Vick and Agent Cobbs opened an investigation on wing, PJ, and Rob. But so far that couldn't prove that they sold drugs, they knew that in some way they were affiliated with one another. Kelly walked in "Hello Shantez, how is the case going?" Agent Vick asked.

Slow motion, not much movement, I really can't say too much as for now! She was trying her best to protect Rob.

What she didn't know was that the agents had been tailing Rob for weeks, and decided that they had enough evidence to opened up their own investigation on him.

Kelly was knee deep, she thought to warn Rob, but if she did she could blow the whole operation and he just might dump her. Kelly's feelings for him had gotten much deeper, she was in love and confused at the same time.

she had to come up with a plan, she just recently found out that she was pregnant. And the thought of an abortion never crossed her mind.

Rob Wing and Jah'me was uptown so they decided to take a drive through their old hood for a couple of minutes. They pulled up on the block that they all started hustling on, Rob was driving the red phantom and Jah'me was riding shot gun.

They bent the corner and all the Hustlers looked in awe, their tints we're so dark that you couldn't tell who was in it! Suddenly the window rolled down slowly and Rob yelled, Soooooowhooooop!" causing every blood in ear shit to run towards his red phantom.

"Damn big homie I didn't know you were eating like this, said the short guy with dreads. Everyone took pictures with Rob. while Jah'me passed out money. Within minutes the entire hood had come out, young Chris walked up to Jah'me and said man, I'm happy as hell, to see a nigga from my hood make it! That's what's up Jah'me said passing the young Hustler a stack.

stay sucka free, Hussle hard, get your weight up and holler back at me whenever you need that brick, and I promise I'll make you a millionaire over night, but the journey starts right here on the block my nigga! He passed him his diamond bracelet. And walked away.

"Be looking for me for me! young Chris yelled.

"I will Jah'me encouraged, as he and Rob jumped back into the phantom, knowing that was going to be the last time they would ever post up in the hood.

Giving back to the hood felt great all together they passed out fifty-stacks and five pounds of exotic weed.

It's something light compared to what we have gained. Jah'me stated, but that giving back shit be feeling good ace! Like you always say Jah'me, you only going to get back, what you put out into the universe. All Facts my nigga all Facts...

Jah'me and Rob had an invitation to paradise island in Miami, they decided to take the fourteen hour road trip in the phantom. After being pulled over twice, once in Ft Lauderdale, and the other in Tampa, Jah'me was frustrated thinking how a black man couldn't drive something nice without being harassed.

Once at the estate, they drove up to the security gate and two giant security guards approached their vehicle, asking who they were their to see.

BK is expecting me! I'm Jah'me. After confirming the invitation, the gates opened slowly, revealing a wonderland full of luxury cars, RVs, and motorcycles.

 "This nigga BK is the real deal. Rob said observing the estate and it's entirety, this estate is breath taking, Rob said. This estate made Jah'mes mansion look like an apartment . And to put the icing on the cake, he had a helicopter sitting just to the right on the lawn. This is the type of money I'm trying to see Jah'me said to Rob.

Good evening the butler said as they arrived to the door. The family awaits your presence in the South Wing! The mansion had marble floors and glass doors with gold door knobs. he also had million dollar paintings, by historical black figures along the wall.

They entered the elevator, headed to the basement where the studio was located, as soon as the elevator opened the aroma of weed hit them in the face, Jah'me a voice yelled!

Ring, Ring, what's happening Luke my boy? "Same shit how you been brother. Shit living bro, living this beautiful blessed life, I just was in California a couple weeks ago, the bitch Diamond and Ms. Phat Phat had niggas dumping all over the place.

Sounds like you all had a ball, we did bro that shit was lit. Can I ask you something Jah'me? Of course Luke he replied back. When do you plan on showing up at the club. To be honest Luke I'm really busy I have a lot on my plate right now, I'm in Florida trying to make a few moves as we speak.

Jah'me when I went into this joint venture with you I did this for you not me! I'm already a multimillionaire. I never did this so you could benefit without showing up and putting in a little work.

I only ask if you could show your face twice a month, so that the big hats would know you, and vouch that you are part owner of the club, and that this is not just a place you launder your money. I have over a hundred and fifty thousand dollars of your money sitting in my safe and you have yet to come pick it up.

Tired of the lecture, he promised to show up the following weekend, he was making large sums of money from the club, but it wasn't like the dope money he consistently brought in.

Dave met up with cuzzo at the local bar and grill, in downtown Washington, DC the bar kept a nice mature crowd and Dave thought it would be a nice spot to talk business privately.

"So you telling me that when you left with the very first shipment, you never got a chance to sell none of the product? "Correct Jah'me and I had a disagreement and whatever he says goes or you can hit the road" so I hit the road "cuzzo replied.

"Kandy vouched for you, so off the strength of her, I'm going to bless you, but I'm going to need a favor!"

"Anything! cuzzo replied. "Well we will see, Dave said smoking his cigar. "Your first shipment will be fifty brick's at twenty-six a piece I don't do shorts. I want every bill you owe me! Get it?

I understand and I promise Im not going to let you down! Cuzzo vowed.

"BK! what's happening? Jah'me said as they embraced, you know my nigga Rob already, of course that's your right hand all day! Facts Jah'me added.

Welcome to my home studio, this is my artist spitta, yeah I met him at my club the night he opened for Jeezy. Oh that's your spot BK asked? Yep Jah'me replied. that's what's up maybe we can throw a album release party their." Man it's whatever Jah'me said excited and optimistic about his future business with BK.

That's a nice phantom you got too. How you know I drove a phantom? Jah'me asked. I saw you coming from five blocks away! Pointing towards his high tech surveillance system . Jah'me told Rob to make a note to invest in that same security system.

As they all took their seats at the round table. How was the drive down 95"? Bk asked. Man the state troopers pulled us over twice! BK started to laugh, man that happens to everyone who drives luxury down here in Florida my guy, but I promise you the next time you come down you will get treated with royalty"

That's what's up Jah'me said. BK stood up and addressed the table. These two men sitting here are my good friends from Virginia, their doing numbers on the east Coast, and I want you all to show them the same love and respect that you show me!

This man here is a made man, he said pointing to Jah'me. That's going to be bringing in a lot of revenue to the family, what we have let no one divide, MBM is the movement.

A woman walked in just as he was finishing up his speech holding a black velvet bag that contained a blue Diamond platinum one hundred caret chain. BK placed it around his neck, "MBM for life my nigga, admiring the million dollar chain, Jah'me said we definitely Motivated By Money my nigga.....

Cuzzo remembered, Luke at the car lot and since he was in D.C and just got blessed, he decided he would go and buy that Bentley that Jah'me promised him, if it was still available.

He pulled up to the luxury lot only to see that his favorite car had been replaced, he walked around hoping, Luke just moved it. Luke walked out of his office and asked if he needed any help. He was shocked when he saw who it was, Cuzzo how you doing? "Im good Luke but whatever happened to my Bentley?

I sold it to Jah'me! He replied.

"How much you want for that Aston Martin?" cuzzo that car is one hundred and fifty thousand dollars Luke told him.

"I'll take it! He cockily said. "what is your means of payment? Luke asked. Opening up his duffle bag Cuzzo shouted out "cash money" revealing stacks of hundreds in the bag. Nice watch Luke told Cuzzo. Yeah it's a Aude Mar!" It definitely is Luke added. Where did you buy it? "Finks in Macy's!

Cuzzo a little advice, this car is way above average, and I don't feel comfortable selling it to a ninteen year old, I don't even drive shit like this.

Cuzzo cut him off, "I want what I want, If it's for sale make it happen! He said to Luke.

Luke sold him the car and a hour later he was pulling off the lot and headed towards highway 664 on his way to the Seven Cities.

Luke filled out the proper paperwork knowing, that the Fed's would have him in no time...

The black and red SR-11 helicopter landed in the parking lot of club strokers, a strip club in Atlanta, Ga. Where only the baddest bitches could grace the stage.

 BK and Jah'me entered the club to a royal V.I.P. welcome. Jah'me was use to getting attention but damn these people were acting as if they were Gods or something.

His new chain caught the eyes of everyone in the club, BK took the mic and welcomed Jah'me to the MBM family. I can get use to this Rob said pouring ace of spades in his glass, not me! Jah'me replied. I knew you were going to say that, Rob said walking away leaving Jah'me to himself.

Cuzzo was uptown Showing out in his new car, he went straight to Joe's tire and rim shop and had a seven-inch lift kit and twenty-Two inch rims put on his new car.

The whole hood came out to see Cuzzo, PJ so happen to be out the hood when he noticed cuzzo, what the fuck! He said to himself. He took out his phone and began to record Cuzzo. Minutes later Cuzzo approached him with his swagger on a million, he also looked like he had invested in more jewelry.

PJ noticed the watch and the bracelet, "Damn, I see you shining boy! " That's what the fuck I do! Cuzzo yelled. "Tell Jah'me I still got love for him, I'm not even mad ace!

He did it to protect the crew, it wasn't nothing towards you. PJ said. "Well I held it down, I ain't no snitch or no bitch ass nigga, you feel me?

PJ started to laugh you still wild as hell, who car you over their fucking up?

"That's my shit nigga, I'm thinking bout copping the Lambo truck next month! By the way I got them joints for the Lizzy too! He said walking away. I hear you PJ said watching his lil-homey pull off. Damn that nigga getting money. Neither one of them noticed agent Vick sitting in the van on the corner.. Fed's taking pictures……

Bk and Jah'me talked about the opportunities that they could invest in, their artist spitta was expected to sell. He had stock in several major corporations, he owned five luxury car lots a Realastate investment firm and three strip clubs. BK had cornered the market he said he brought in five-million a month in investments, and twenty million a month in drugs, he even offered Jah'me his mansion in Ga, because he didn't want him to live where he laid his head, Jah'me took his advice and made future plans to move to GA.

Until then BK wanted to take the helicopter to see the Mayweather fight in Vegas. Once they arrived they were escorted to the dressing room where Floyd was warming up.

Money making Mayweather BK yelled! "whats good BK. Mayweather greeted. Shit came to see my main man in action. This my man Jah'me, he apart of the MBM family now! They both shook and greeted one another. Jah'me started laughing because he was just watching a old Mayweather fight when he cuzzo and Kandy went on the road trip to DC, it's just funny how the universe operates he thought to himself.

Now let's get down to business! BK said. Jah'me had a confused look on his face . I bet the fight don't go six rounds for a million cash, I bet you two million I drop his ass in five. That's a bold bet! BK replied. No nuts no glory! Floyd boasted and aren't you tired of donating your money to me? Bet your wraith too? Mayweather said cockily. BK Backed off, you already have three of my rides and I'm going to get them back too!

Not if you keep betting against me! Mayweather placing his bet on FanDuel, they got it going the whole twelve so I'm going to bet I put to sleep for a hundred grand, that's crazy he actually betting on himself, I got to see this unfold, we about to take our seats good luck champ. All Hussle no luck he replied back!!

You know I don't believe in that luck shit! Mayweather said. I believe in destiny and I'm destined to be the greatest ever to do this!! I like that BK said walking out. I love the hell out of the nigga. Facts Jah'me added.

Why y'all be betting? Jah'me asked. "something to do. BK replied back..

Cuzzo was going hard in the paint word on the street was that he had the hood on lock. PJ told Rob everything he heard in the streets. He even showed him the video of Cuzzo. Man this boy doing donuts in a two hundred thousand dollar car, Rob said laughing. Make sure you stay far away from him. I hear you PJ replied.

Meanwhile back at his condo, Kandy had been his personal sex slave for many hours of the day. After Popping triple stacks, drinking, and snorting powder, Kandy's physical health wasn't good, she was starting to look bad, whenever she would ask cuzzo for food, he would give her more powder to snort.

He had her where he wanted her, he played highly on her emotional state and took advantage of her. She soon became dependent on him. Meanwhile agent Cobbs was outside. Fed's taking pictures...

Cuzzo received a call from David early Saturday morning, after a long night of drugs and sex, David was the last person he wanted to talk to!

Do you remember the favor I said you owe me? It

is that time my friend. I'm not going to talk on this phone so I'm flying in on Sunday. I will call you from a disclose location where we will meet up and go over the details, don't let me down man!David said.

"All I have is my word and my balls! "Cuzzo said hanging up wondering what the hell David had up his sleeve.

Back at the federal headquarters Vick and Cobbs finally had put their case together they had a black board set up with pictures of the crew lines up by rank and responsibility's. The first picture was Rob, beside his name read lieutenant. PJ, Wing, and Cuzzo's pictures all had workers beside them. And Jah'mes picture was at the bottom as unknown suspect.

What we have here ….Vick began " they are selling crack, heroin, and prescription narcotics in our urban District, right under our nose. Our records date back five years. These thugs have been selling drugs, since they were fifteen, sixteen, and fucking seventeen years old.

 Baby's one agent said out loud! in age they are, But their old heads in these streets. We have enough evidence to convict them all on conspiracy and money Laundering. But the goal is to catch them Dirty. Let's get back on the beat, we have a organized drug ring to bust! Be safe and good luck!

David's plane landed at Norfolk international airport Sunday morning. After renting his luxury vehicle he drove down military highway to meet up with cuzzo at IHOP.

He sat near the window where he could observe everyone who entered, he order a coffee all black and a cheese omelet, as soon as he began to eat he heard a loud noise coming from outside sounding like thunder, it was Cuzzo pulling in blasting his music.

David hated seeing black men act so ignorant with money. "what up Dee? My name is David! He corrected. Whatever man let's just get down to business ace!

David handed him a brown paper bag, Don't open it until you leave from out of here. Cuzzo shook it as if he was checking for a bomb! David shook his head at the notion. It contains money, keys and a map of the estate of the person I want you to kill. The combination to the panic room is 983. No excuses!

Damn Dee you want me to body a nigga?

You owe me big time, cuzzo!"

"I know and I got you!" he said looking confused. He then handed cuzzo a round trip plane ticket, departure time read 5:45 pm. "A gun will be under the toilet seat in the guest bathroom downstairs. Our target is expecting to be home around 11 pm.

Cuzzo shook his head and stormed out! minutes later David got up, paid his tab and left.

He never spotted the agents, running his tags and following him back to his hotel.....

Rob arrived to the airport around noon. He walked towards the flight board and noticed that Jah'mes flight was due to land in minutes. After standing at gate 11 for over twenty minutes, he walked over to ask the attendant was his flight delayed? She type some commands into her computer and confirmed that his flight was delayed and was set to land an hour.

Rob decided to stretch his legs and walk around a little. He seen and approached a nice looking brown skinned woman, drinking Starbucks and listening to her music, he kindly introduced himself.

She said her name was Kira and she was a college student part time flight attendant, and that she was working to pay for her food, rent and school books.

she went on complaining about being broke and not ever having enough money, after listening for more than ten minutes straight, Rob didn't know if, it was a cry out for help, or if she was selling pussy So He leaned forward and whispered something in her ear..

The car is rented to a David Bank's, the woman at the Enterprise rental told agent Vick. Agent Cobbs walked in, with a print out of his rap sheet, he is from Miami, FL. With prior drug charges, He did a five-year Federal stretch at New Jersey's fort Dix on drug charges. The agents gave each other a high five the finally had the Plug!

Jah'mes plane landed thirty minutes later. He existed through gate 11 expecting to see Rob, He was nowhere to be found, He dialed his number and as soon as he, hit the call button, his phone went completely dead! Damn he shook his head at the notion the he had been playing the game on his phone so long that he killed his Battery.

Grabbing his suitcase from the turn style, he began to walk towards the exit door's. He noticed two cabs and immediately waved down the first. As soon as he was about to give the Mexican driver his home address, he noticed the red phantom two cars up. A big yellow bus had pulled away exposing the luxury vehicle.

Jah'me gave the driver a twenty and existed the cab. He walked over surveying the vehicle, making sure it belonged to him, observing the thirty day tags, and listening to the lil-baby banging through the speakers. He knew at that moment it was Rob so he opened the door, only to see Rob getting some exclusive head! It had to be, because this nigga was sweating like a runaway slave and crawling up the seat.

What up bro! as you can see I got cha, a home coming present bitch!! she your type too chocolate cute, and thick as hell. They ran a train on Kira right in the loading area of the airport.

After they finish, she and Rob exchanged numbers and he passed her two thousand dollars. Damn you really liked that pussy ace, Jah'me said. it was alright she just been down on her luck lately, and I wanted to help her out. By fucking her Jah'me asked? Laughing. how much you pay her? Something light!! Rob replied back, Reebok money....

Washington, DC was cold and crisp and the rain didn't make it any better. Cuzzo arrived at the estate around eight pm. Dressed in all black, with his map and instructions.

He jumped the wall and walked around the back to

let himself in. Once in he went straight to the security room, where he could retrieve any video's that were recording him entering or leaving, after unplugging the entire system, he headed upstairs.

He only had a couple of minutes before the target was due to arrive. He walked to the master suit, and entered the code, access granted! he quickly loaded his Glock nine, and sat on the bed, nervous and scared, but this had to be done.

Vick and Cobbs called and got in contact with the agents in Florida. After discovering David had just violated his probation by leaving the city without telling his probation officer, they could arrest him and hold him for questioning.

The Florida DEA taskforce was faxed and their plans was to execute a raid on David's home within the next twenty four hours.

"Get the fuck! out of here Jah'me said looking at the video of cuzzo. "You said, he said that he had em for the low? PJ confirmed.

 Who in they right mind would front cuzzo that much work? More or less y'all know to stick to the strip. I know y'all love him and I do as well, but for the sake of our freedom, stay far away from lil-cuzz.

He walked away reminding himself that he needed to make a surprise visit.

Deon pulled in, driving his baby blue Royals Royce wraith, with the white rag top. He and his family had just left an event earlier and had plans on making it a movie night. Cuzzo watched them as they pulled in, he began practicing shooting the gun towards the door.

He had never shot anyone in his nineteen years, and he was as nervous as he'd ever been before. Dontes wife went to tuck their infant son Cam'ron in for the night. Donte proceeded to walked towards the master suite, he felt something was amiss, but he quickly brushed it off.

He opened the door and stood "shocked at what appeared to be cuzzo, in all black pointing a gun in his direction.

The club had a buzz and everyone was their showing out their newest rides and latest fashion's Dj Kalid and Drama both rocked the house while kay slay hosted the event.

Jah'me and his crew entered and headed straight to V.I.P. and were quickly served bottles of champagne. All eyes were glued to them. Everybody wanted to know just who they were, Luke walked up surprised to see Jah'me.

"Whats good luke?'

Business! he replied back.

'Excuse us! Luke said pulling Jah'me to the side, he sat and told him everything that went down with cuzzo. I just wish you hadn't sold him that car. "Are you serious? Luke shouted. I hadn't sold a car in a week and he comes along and buys the most expensive one I have. Jah'me began to laugh.

What's so funny? Luke asked. It was Jah'mes turn to tell Luke about Cuzzo's wild behavior. Get outta here! Luke said shocked. That's just cuzzo Jah'me said.

But since you're here let's handle business, he pulled out his check book and wrote Jah'me a check one hundred and twenty thousand dollars.

"That's your cut for the week!' Luke informed.

"That's a lot of money, Luke!

No that's the results of a smart investment!' Luke said. And there is more million's to be made! Jah'me walked away shaking his head deep in thought, thinking of ways he could invest his money and finally leave the game.

"Cuzzo, what the fuck you doing with that gun? I didn't want this cuzzo said. Is it money you want

Deon asked? I have a couple of million in the stash. Just don't kill me man I got my family in the next room he begged!

Fuck your money I ain't broke nigga! Cuzzo closed his eyes and shot Donte twice in the arm, and jumped out the bed room window.

Donte's wife ran in screaming what happened? Call an ambulance cuzzo just tried to kill me, I'm going to have my cousin handle his ass..

Rob found out that Kelly was four months Pregnant, happy as hell to be a first time dad, he made plans to throw her an extravagant over the top baby shower.

Jah'me had yet to meet her and Rob wanted to make sure he introduced his best friend to his soon to be wife.

But Jah'me and Kelly both were always busy and on the move, and from the way things were looking, they would eventually meet, at the wedding...

Kelly was back in her office going over Robs files. She noticed all he had, on his criminal record was a misdemeanor possession and two speeding tickets.

She also noticed that he had a high school diploma, along with three years of ITT Technical school. After learning all of this she fell deeper in love with Rob. Damn she said to herself I'm in love with a thug!

PJ, Jah'me, and Rob decided to eat at Captain George's. Once in the restaurant they noticed someone was circling the phantom. From a distance it looked to be cuzzo. They all walked out towards the car.

"I thought that was y'all! Cuzzo said laughing. That phantom is nasteeee!

"What do you want cuzzo. Jah'me asked.

"I want some love nigga, we blood. And how could y'all even think I would tell on my crew? Y'all sure y'all not getting high. The fuck up Jah'me replied back, How did you get out so fast cuzzo? "man on big momma, I don't know. What I do know is I ain't tell them cracker's shit!

Think about it, seriously Jah' I know everything about you we cousins dick head! If I snitched why the hell are you still walking around this bitch free as a bird? Cuzzo asked.

He then reached into his coat pocket and was quickly ambushed by the crew, pointing their guns at him. Y'all be easy!

He pulled out a old picture, when he was seven

and they were nine, they were all Up-Town sitting on the basketball court drinking soda's, eating pickle's and sunflower seeds. Candy lady penny on up bitch! They all looked at the picture and began to laugh, those were the good ole days, we were NFL then and were NFL now! Cuzzo said. can a nigga get some fucking love? Jah'me hugged and decided to forgive his cousin.

"Get in! we're going to go eat at Little Daddy's, we made a scene out her Jah'me said observing the people looking out the windows.

What about my car cuzzo asked? We will come back for it Rob replied.

Not once did they notice agent Cobbs sitting across the street. Fed's taking pictures.

Little Daddy's was a soul food restaurant on princess Ann road. It's could be busy on any particular day, because they cooked food, sold drugs, cut hair and washed cars all out of one building.

Ms. Emma worked for Little Daddy's for over three years, and knew most of the customers, and Jah'me was always V.I.P.

Hey handsome! I know you like to face the door, so I'm going to go clear your table right now! "Thank you Mrs Emma minutes later they were all sitting at the table when Jah'me asked cuzzo, so why they say they let you out again?

He told Jah'me everything from the day he was arrested, to the present day. He admitted to buying that car only because he knew that Jah'me would hear about it!

But that was stupid ? Jah'me replied. You only live once cuzzo added. I know y'all didn't expect me to fall off like freak draws cuz, not after being spoiled my entire life.

Upstairs Rob was sitting on the toilet rolling a blunt while observing the parking lot, he saw various types of people admiring the phantom.

He also seen a yellow cab sitting to the far right, he noticed the driver was wearing shades and kept ducking his head every time someone would exist the restaurant.

 Rob being the smart man he was, knew something wasn't right, after further investigation he came up with one thing and one thing only the fucking FED'S!

He rushed downstairs and told Jah'me, what he witnessed, Jah'me had Ms. Emma escort them out the back door, where Wing was waiting.

Go to the spot, call everyone, they all need to be their in ten minutes. Jah'me instructed. I got you Rob said shaking his head at Cuzzo's hot ass!

Ms. Emma's Chrysler 300 was the last car to leave the parking lot, she walked out and loaded her trunk with the left over food, from today's menu to drop off at the local shelter.

She noticed agent Cobbs sitting in a cab, this time he was parked behind the phantom. Agent Cobbs knew that she had something to do with the disappearance of the crew, because he didn't see neither one of them leave the building.

He called Vick and Kelly and minutes later they were all on the scene with the forensic unit, and a warrant to search the phantom.

Agent Cobb retrieved from the car an ounce of weed, a Glock nine, and an expensive necklace that was in a jewelry box case.

"what do we have here? Vick asked walking over.

Nothing much just your typical dope boy package.

Agent Vick looked at the necklace and said this just might be the case that will break the bank! Holding the chain in the air. MBM! That sounds fimilure! Kelly said.

MBM means motivated by money! Out of Houston, TX. I see a big promotion coming for us all.

Everyone accept cuzzo had shown up, He decided to go his own way he knew Jah'me and Rob still wasn't feeling him. Jah'me was pacing back and forth on the apartment floor, pass the EL! He said to PJ Everyone was quite.

No need to look all crazy now" y'all know the count! We hot and Fed's are on to us and theirs nothing we can do about it! Jah'me phone ring and it was BK. We have a problem to handle. can I call you back? Jah'me asked.No this can't wait, you cousin tried to kill my people's in DC! BK informed Jah'me that Deon was his cousin! He said he knew you too and that the only person who had the pass codes to his home was David, they have been having some money issues lately, so David went his way a couple weeks ago!

We think cuzzo was hired to sell his dope and to kill Deon. So it's going to get real ugly if you don't handle this situation before I do!

David or cuzzo? Jah'me asked.

Both! BK replied and hung up

Jah'me threw his phone towards the wall.

Everyone just sat quiet as he paced the floor. He called Rob into to the kitchen.

Man we crumbling ace! The walls are closing in, and cuzzo then got into some more shit." BK wants him dead. He began to tell Rob all of Cuzzo's devious deeds, PJ and Wing eavesdrop on the conversation and shook their heads. Jah'me called them into the kitchen.

Y'all know I love y'all till the death of me. I told y'all from the beginning that this game don't love nobody.

 The Fed's are on to us and I don't have one day for them cracker's, I'm leaving on the first flight, after I talk to cuzzo and I suggest you all do the same.

Rob should have a care package for you ready by ten and make sure y'all meet him on time we don't have that luxury anymore, time is definitely not on our side. The money I'm giving y'all should hold you for awhile! Jah'me said hugging his crew.

I'll see you again for sure! He and Rob existed the condo, before getting into the rental Jah'me told Rob to book him a ticket first flight smoking to London!

What about the mansion? Rob asked. " fuck it bro! The Fed's going to have it soon, they both headed to the estate to empty all six safes.

The D.E.A in Florida we're seconds from kicking in the door! They were just waiting on the green light. David had only been back home a couple of hours when he heard a loud Boom! DEA Don't move or I will blow your fucking brains out!

 David was handcuffed and detained. After searching the house they discovered 1.2 million in cash three bricks of heroin, and a duffle bag full of guns. The agents were sure that they had their man......

Agents Kelly, Vick, and Cobbs showed up on the scene, they had pictures of the crew, Kelly or the other agents had seen Jah'me accept in the club picture, so they brushed him off the supplier list or the main connect.

They took his picture off of the suspect board and bawled it up. Happy to hear about David's arrest they let their guard down, unaware that they had just thrown in trashed the picture of the leader of the N.F.L crew..

"Man I'm going to miss this big ass house! "Rob said grabbing money out of the safe, divided equally, They each had a million dollars apiece, he walked out never looking back as he passed the Bentley, and phantom.

Jah'me pulled up to Cuzzo's condo around ten that night, Jah'me noticed his car had a flat tire and a dent in the hood. Kandy's car was right beside his, they both had been up getting high and fucking for a week.

Who is it! Cuzzo yelled.

"Jah'me Phew!

Cuzzo put on a robe and opened the door. Kandy hadn't seen Jah'me in over a year. She didn't want him to see her strung out so she stayed hidden in the room.

What's going on Cuzz? Cuzzo asked. I get a call from Bk, saying you tried to kill Donte the other day, what's up with that?

Cuzzo was hoping Kandy hadn't heard that, but she heard everything.

"Yeah and so! The fuck you mean so!! he wants you dead. He has a hit out on you, I'm just here to warn you, better haul ass out of town if you know like I do!

You not even built to kill nobody! Jah'me told him. Cuzzo walked around and opened the kitchen drawer, he retrieve the nine millimeter and walked around to where Jah'me was standing.

"phew I'm built for whatever phew! You always looked out for other niggas that won't our blood more than you did blood. He was referring to Rob.

That's because you a fuck up! You the whole reason our operation went down!

So you calling me a snitch? Cuzzo asked still pointing his gun at Jah'me. You better shoot me because If you don't,,

"What nigga? Cuzzo said waving his gun aggressively in Jah'mes face. You think I won't kill you Jah'me? Beg for your life nigga!

Jah'me looked cuzzo square in the eye and said, I swear on Big Mama's grave, that I'm going to kill you if you don't kill me!!

Cuzzo laughed and bit his lip Boom!!!!!!

Rob pulled up and seen the crew waiting, he passed each of them a duffle bag. Jah'me said that is for your loyalty and nothing else. He also told me to tell you all to get out of VA. Wing said he was headed up top. PJ said, he was planning on leaving but he had to bless his mom and his two b/M's first.

They all embrace vowing to meet back up soon,

once shit cools down.

"IF you ever in New York get with me! I won't be hard to find I will be at the Garden! I'm buying season tickets, I'll be close to Spike! that's what's up I'll be sure to tell Jah'me, Rob said pulling out of the parking lot.

Kandy stood over Cuzzo's dead body with a smoking gun in her hands. Jah'me walked over and embraced her, it's ok baby we got to get the fuck out of here, they fled and within minutes you could hear the police sirens coming from a distance, just as they exited the neighborhood, the police were entering.

Jah'me thanked Kandy for saving his life, and whatever the fuck cuzzo was on had took over his mind.

He looked over at Kandy and realized that she had lost big weight and looked strung out. I got to get you some help he said headed to the hotel.

Rob was their awaiting his arrival shocked as hell to see him walk in with Kandy! The look on Jah'me face told him something was wrong, he walked over and rolled a backwood and poured a shot of Hennessy. Looking over the plan ticket's he explained to Rob how cuzzo died, Rob shook his head in disbelief, he was going to go either way!

Jah'me said.

Rob just sat and listened as his phone began to vibrate. It was a Text from Kelly, it read (Can you meet me at Have a Nice Day Café in waterside asap) He told Jah'me that everything was a go and that the flight to London was scheduled to leave in two hours, and that he needed to make one more stop before they left. I have to say bye to Kelly she's at waterside.

Man too many police be downtown ace! we probably all over the news and shit! I don't think that is a good idea bro!

I'll be ok, in and out! you already know the count ace. He said to Jah'me giving him dapp. He walked away and drove off into the night.....

PJ was shooting dice and smoking a blunt on Bagnall Rd. when Suddenly a black Tahoe pulled up, and a mob of federal agents jumped out pointing their guns in his direction. All he could say was damn I should have listened to Jah'me.........

Rob walked in and saw Kelly sitting at the bar. Eating without me? He asked. You took forever she replied. I'm not hungry anyway. I just wanted to see your beautiful face, some shit hit the fan and me and my crew have to flee the city for a minute.

"So when will I hear back from you? You know I'm six months now."

"I know baby. Just trust me, I will always keep in contact with you. Rob's phone rings and it's Jah'me. He let it ring because he was kissing Kelly, just know I will always love you no matter what happens Kelly said. She then excused herself to the ladies room.

Rob called Jah'me back. Hello? How long you going to be? He asked. He never heard a response, all he heard was DEA, get in the ground.

That bitch set me up...

Vick and Cobbs both reported to the scene, where cuzzo laid dead with a gun in his hand, the lead detective said it was a homicide.

Cuzzo had two hundred thousand worth of drugs and guns in his condo. Nothing was missing or out of place. They found a jacket with a picture stuffed in the pocket. The agents recognized everyone and thought that they may have been wrong about Jah'me, but they once again wrote it off. Vick walked over and showed Cobbs an empty gun.

"Why would he grab the empty gun, when all the other ones were fully loaded?

Maybe he was trying to scare somebody. And if he

pulled his gun out he knew, that person wouldn't kill him right? He was killed from his blindside, he never saw it coming, so it had to be at least two or more people.

But why not take the money and the drugs, since it was visible? Agent Vick asked.

Because it was Pocket change to whoever killed him. Agent Cobbs answered.........

"We have to leave now Kandy Rob just got busted!

How? She asked. I don't know the details but we out! I told him not to go. Jah'me called a Uber and headed straight to Norfolk international, scared for his life, they drove over the campostell bridge and Jah'me threw the smoking gun Kandy had and phone out, vowing that he would never see the city again.

Rob was back at the head quarters getting debriefed. "we know everything about you! Agent Vick yelled. "So why the fuck am I here? Rob asked. "To save yourself from sixty to life, we got a whole laundry list of charge's let's start with money Laundering, conspiracy, murder, but you can help yourself by helping us!

"Man help this dick! And take me to the Jail I'm tired of talking. Oh you tuff huh? Agent Vick asked.

Till the wheels fall off!!

The air was cold and rainy and the city was crowded, London was nothing like the States, people drove on the opposite side of the road and shit.

Jah'me and Kandy lived in a exclusive pad, with live in butler's and maids. Money was never an issue because he was worth more than five-million dollar's, and his checks from Luke continue to come through for him weekly.

His main goal was to get Rob the best lawyer money could buy and hopefully he had a second chance at life.

PJ decided to fight his case, it ended up getting put off, a year pending further investigation. PJ sent word that he was good. And that he saw on the news about cuzzo being dead.

At first he thought BK had a hit put out on him. But when he heard it wasn't a forced entry, And that cuzzo had been shot once in his head. He thought Jah'me did it...

Rob was hand cuffed to the table when agent Kelly walked in. He shook his head in disappointment, what the fuck you doing here I'm not trying to talk to your police ass!

let me help you, I love you and know exactly how you can beat this whole case, but you have to trust and believe me!'

Why should I ? Rob asked. "She pointed to her stomach and said because we need you. And she began to explain to Rob the federal case laws to look up and give to his lawyer.

Kandy had gotten her weight back and was starting to look like her old self again. Six months had passed since Rob's arrest. Things had cooled down, so Jah'me and Kandy decided to fly out to see the Celtics play the Knicks and do a little shopping. Their plane was leaving at noon.

Rob's court date had come and his plea bargain was fifty years. He was dressed in his Armani custom tailor suit, Gator leather shoes, and he sported a custom Rolex presidential. His confidence and aura was felt throughout the court room as if he had a worry in the world.

His trial was high profile and was aired locally, and state wide. The DA wanted a conviction on conspiracy, since they couldn't prove murder. Rob thought it was over, until his lawyer objected and said the agent working this investigation had sexual relations with his client and was currently pregnant with his child.

Kelly was called up to take the stand. "Is it true that you are a federal agent working this investigation, and that you are pregnant with the defendants child?

Yes your honor I am! The court room erupted in a uproar " "order in the court "order in the court. Bailiff arrest agent Kelly and charged her! The judge ordered. He continued knowing the world was watching, " Smith v Shelby 1997 any agent federal or state cannot engage sexually with any suspect. if so the case is deemed non valid and all charges are immediately dropped. "Mr. Davis your case is dismissed and you are free to go!

Jah'me and Kandy had been shopping all day in the lower Eastside. Kandy's feet were starting to hurt, as much as these shoes cost my feet shouldn't be hurting like this she said.

Jah'me started laughing, we can finish up Sunday before we leave. He walked in the middle of the street and flagged down the first cab he saw. He directed the cab to the plaza hotel! And please Take the long route me and my woman would like to enjoy the sights. The driver hit his meter and happily obliged.

"Mr. Davis one reporter yelled! "Yes Rob said smiling. How does it feel to be a free man?

" It feels good phew! Justice was served and my innocence was proven, now I can go live a blessed and productive life with my family, thank you all for believing in justice, stay blessed and positive. He entered the passenger side of the Rang Rover, leaving the court room in shock and the Fed's mad as hell....

PJ was watching TV when the breaking news flash came across the screen, Drug kingpin set free due to improper investigation by federal agent. Rob was then shown coming out the court room smiling.

The reporter went on to say that justice wasn't being served, and as long as people like Robert Davis was a free man, the Streets would continue to be infested with high crime rates, drugs, and murderers. Is this what our tax dollars are paying for? I suggest you call your local Congress man before the rest of the thugs begin to walking out of the prison's and jails.

PJ started to celebrate knowing it was over, he called Brocoletti, his lawyer. He had just heard of his codefendants release and said he should be released also within the hour.

PJ was happy as hell, walking back to his cell, he yelled y'all can have all this shit! he pointed to the large bags of commissary and cloths on his bed………

Kandy undressed and walked towards the door. Damn you sexy! Jah'me said. Whatever! she said with a shy grin. Jah'me sparked a blunt and turned the television to CNN, Breaking news! a Virginia kingpin set free today next!

He continued smoking throughout the commercial, but when he saw Rob walk out of the courtroom he had to adjust his eyes, he thought the weed was playing tricks on his mind.

Seeing Rob free was like he had been reborn. Kandy came running in at all the commotion and was told about Rob's release, she began screaming!! as Jah'me popped open a bottle of champagne, making a toast to love, loyalty, and the release of a Real Gangster. He made plans to fly out to the city in two days.

PJ was released an hour later and was picked up by bump beezy, Jah'mes youngest cousin and a well known gangster! Where you going buzzo? Take me home my ganster! Once at his house he went directly to where he hid his money, and dug it up, he retrieve five bands and buried the rest. as soon as he bent the corner agent Cobbs and Agent Vick were standing in front of his house.

You think you got off free huh? He stood silent, he didn't want to give them any reason to search him, he had only been out two hours.

He just wanted them to go away as soon as possible, I got my eye on your black ass! The first time you slip I'm going to be the one who put them cuffs around your wrist, with that being said they both got back in their squad car and drove away!

The alarm awakened Kandy and Jah'me from their rest. It was 9:30 and the game was starting at 10:30 get dressed before we be late Kandy.

Once they arrived at the garden, it was the end of the first quarter, and Boston was up by twelve so he wasn't even tripping.

He sat down beside Jayson Tatum's mother. It was so funny hearing her cheer for her son. It seem like every thing he shot was wet. Boston won 105-85 Kandy noticed spike Lee sitting on the other side of the basketball court.

Bae don't that couple sitting next to Spike Lee look just like Wing and Bon-Bon? After focusing his eyes he agreed. He yelled at the top of his lungs wing!!!!

Wing had definitely heard his name and he began to look In several directions. They met in the middle of the basketball court, Happy as hell to see each other they embraced and together headed back to the hotel.

Kelly was sentenced to eighteen months and one day. She was to serve out the entirety of her sentence at the women's federal facility in Maryland.

She would later give birth to a beautiful baby girl name Nichole. Rob was granted full custody, He and Nichole visited Kelly every weekend, until her release. The facility informed her that funds was at it's max after Rob deposited another twenty thousand into her Jpay account.

Back at the hotel, they all sat at the round table just like old times. It has been over a year since they last saw one another. Wing and Bon-Bon had gotten married and lived in an exclusive estate in Raleigh, NC where they owned a health care business, along with several other investments.

 Jah'me went on to tell him about Robs and Cuzzo's situation and that he was cleared to go back home if he wanted too. It just all seem unreal! wing replied. Shit how you think I feel Jah'me replied back excited! Get some rest cuzz, our flight leave in the morning.

Jah'me observed Kandy standing on the balcony

over looking the beautiful New York skyline. She asked, how does it feel to be a free man, Jah'me? "Like my man Rob said it feels good Phew.

After Kelly's sentence was over her and Rob reunited outside the gates of the prison, along with Their daughter Nichole was now seven months.

Kelly was so happy to be reunited with her family, she had gained thirty pounds, and looked totally different than she did when she left. Rob was loving the thickness with a passion. Kelly couldn't wait to launch her clothing line, she came up with in prison.

Along with her private investigator company, she still had connections in law enforcement, making Rob's drug empire a lot more organized and powerful.

PJ Owned a couple of car lots on VA, beach Blvd. He had turned a new leaf and decided to leave the game alone. He loved the town to much to relocate, after all he was already rich!

Jah'me and Kandy decided to leave the states to raise their expected twin boys Jaylen, and Jah'mille in Africa. He didn't want them to have to grow up living in his street life image, and knowing that he was a Kingpin, He just wanted more for his boy's, he was looking forward to a new life full of business investments, and Realastate ventures.

He heard Cape Town South Africa was on the come up. He just wanted the best outcome for his family, and prayed that one day his past wouldn't catch up with his future, But then again he always prepared himself for the unthinkable.

Agent Cobbs and Agent Vick continues to investigating the N.F.L. Crew........

You just read Another Up-Town CLASSIC, be on the lookout for Kandy PT 3 Jah'mille's Rage...

Made in the USA
Middletown, DE
10 July 2022

68930606R00076